MURDER IN THE SNOW

Carl and the girl were at the gate, Carl pushing it open, the snow mounded on either side of the narrow pathway that had been cleared but was now iced over . . .

Bounty hunter Craig Chappell was about to drop his head, keep walking, and double back. Then he saw Brown at the window, a gun raised in his hand. Now everything speeded up.

Chappell shouted at Carl and burst through the gate at the same time. Carl turned to him, losing his balance, the girl screaming as Carl slipped, Chappell coming up face to face with him as the gun went off, making a little popping sound as the glass in the window shattered.

Three-hundred-pound Carl took the bullet in the back of his head and fell, dead weight now, into the snow, crushing Chappell beneath him.

Chappell pushed at the dead body, reaching for the gun in his pocket. He looked at the window. Brown was gone . . .

Books by John Leslie

Blood on the Keys
Bounty Hunter Blues

Published by POCKET BOOKS

BOUNTY HUNTER
Blues

JOHN LESLIE

POCKET BOOKS

New York   London   Toronto   Sydney   Tokyo   Singapore

For John Thomson

An *Original* Publication of POCKET BOOKS

POCKET BOOKS, a division of Simon & Schuster Inc.
1230 Avenue of the Americas, New York, NY 10020

ISBN: 1-416-59868-5 ISBN: 978-1-416-59868-5

First Pocket Books printing June 1990

10 9 8 7 6 5 4 3 2 1

BOUNTY HUNTER
Blues

_____ *One*

*C*RAIG CHAPPELL FIRST HEARD ABOUT HIS BROTHER Barry's death from the Montreal Urban Community police. Craig had sent Barry up there a week ago to track down and bring back a guy who'd skipped the country with a hundred-thousand-dollar bond hanging over his head.

When the homicide detective from MUC called, Craig was at his office in downtown Miami, playing back the tape of an X-rated conversation made from an illegal wiretap. Barry had bugged the private phone of a woman who lived in a condo on Biscayne

Boulevard a couple of weeks earlier. In that time they'd heard plenty of conversations, but the ones they were interested in were those between the guy Barry was after in Montreal, John Brown, and the woman whose phone was bugged, Brown's girlfriend in Miami.

Craig picked up the phone and listened as the homicide detective in Montreal identified himself.

"I'd like to speak to Craig Chappell," the detective said.

"Speaking," Craig said. He was aware of his heart pounding. Listening to the conversation recorded last night between midnight and 12:45, his heartbeat had been doing triple time; listening to the homicide detective provided a different kind of excitement.

"I'm calling about Barry Chappell. Any relation?"

"My brother," Craig said.

"I'm sorry to have to tell you that he's dead, shot last night here in Montreal."

Craig took a deep breath. He felt numb, unable to think. It was the kind of phone call everyone dreaded. Whether it came in the middle of the night or the middle of the day, it didn't matter. It had the same effect.

He should have gone to Canada instead of Barry. These kinds of assignments, he felt, were his responsibility. Not because he didn't have confidence in his brother, but because he always played it cautious. Barry got the easier pickups, the ones Craig thought presented the least danger. But they never came with any guarantees. Some kid decides to jump bond after stealing his first car, and you happen to find him on a day when he's high on crack—then anything can happen.

Before Craig was supposed to leave for Montreal

there was a sudden break in another case they had been working on. A guy who'd been arrested for embezzlement of funds at a Miami insurance office where he'd once worked was released on bond, and two days later walked into the office and opened fire with a twelve-gauge shotgun he'd carried in beneath his raincoat. He killed his boss, the female receptionist, and a coworker before tucking the shotgun back under the raincoat and casually walking back out to the street. The lead Craig got was from one of his sources. There was a guy living at a fancy hotel on the beach who paid a week in advance in cash every Friday, lived on room service and carryout joints with delivery.

When Craig made some calls to a few other hotels in Miami, he found a pattern. A guy checked in late at night with a reservation, paid a week in advance, and sometimes—but not always—had it extended for another week. After spending a day on the telephone with most of Miami's big and medium-sized hotels, Craig thought he had it narrowed down. He arranged the dates in chronological order. Unless the hermit had been doing this in other places in the country, or there were hotels Craig had missed, the guy started this pattern at the Fontainebleau, on Miami Beach, the night of the insurance murders.

It was too good to pass up. Once the police got it—and he was surprised they hadn't already—Craig would lose out on the $25,000 the bonding agency was paying for the hermit's capture. Friday was the day the hermit's bill was due. It was also the day Craig was supposed to leave for Montreal.

Barry got the Montreal assignment.

Craig went to the hotel on Friday and made the easiest tag of his life. The guy was practically begging

3

to be caught. When Craig knocked on the door and called the guy by his real name, the hermit said, "What took you so long?"

"What time?" Craig asked.
"What?" the detective asked.
"What time did he die?"
"Around one o'clock this morning."
"How did it happen?"
"We think he was entering an apartment when he was shot twice with a .45-caliber weapon."

Craig didn't say anything, listened to the dead air between Canada and Miami, sure the cop would go on, relieved when he did.

"The neighbors called us," the detective continued. "Somebody heard the shots. When we got there we found your brother."

Craig looked out the window of his office, at the spire of the courthouse, and three floors below, on the street, the small offices with signs outside advertising bail bonds.

"And no leads, right," Craig said.

"We thought you might help us there," the detective said. "We saw your brother's ID. He was working, wasn't he?"

Craig swallowed coffee that had turned cold in his cup. "Yeah, he was working."

"Who was he after?"

"A guy named John Brown."

"That's not much," the detective said. Craig thought he heard the beginning traces of sarcasm in his voice. Still, after finding a dead American bounty hunter, with no legal authority, on his doorstep, this guy was being more polite than his American counterpart would have been under similar circumstances.

"It's about all I've got," Craig said. "The guy skipped out on his bond down here."

There was another long silence. "What do you want to do about your brother?"

"I'll come up and get him."

"Good. We'd like to talk to you."

Craig sat for a moment staring at the tape recorder. They had talked for half an hour, sometimes longer, a couple times a week. Jeannie, the girlfriend, sounded like she couldn't care less that Brown was a fugitive who had skipped the country on a hundred-thousand-dollar bond. All she seemed to be interested in was when he was coming home. Some of the calls got personal, really personal.

Like the one last night recorded between midnight and 12:45. Craig had listened to it once this morning and rewound it to play again after talking to the detective in Montreal. The first time he heard the tape, he had thought what a kick Barry would get out of it.

Craig stood up, poured himself fresh coffee from the pot on the two-burner hot plate before punching the play button on the recorder. The excitement was gone; he was listening now for information, something he might have missed the first time around that could be useful. He sat back down in the swivel chair and put his feet up on the desk. There was the sound of a phone ringing and then a woman's sleepy voice answered.

Woman: Hello.

Brown: Jeannie, did I wake you?

Jeannie: John? (The woman yawning) What time is it?

Brown: After midnight.

5

Jeannie: What are you doing?

Brown: I'm in bed.

Jeannie: (Giggling) Alone?

Brown: If you don't count the Colt under my pillow.

Jeannie: You're kinky.

Brown: Yeah. You wanna make love?

Jeannie: Over the phone?

Brown: You got a better way with me in Montreal and you down in Miami?

Jeannie: I've never done it on the phone.

Brown: It's easy. I'll tell you everything to do. What have you got on?

Jeannie: My nightgown.

Brown: Take it off.

There was silence. Craig knew what was coming next, how it was going to end, but it didn't arouse him. He just sat staring at the tape recorder, angry, thinking how stupid he'd been. Listening now, but not listening.

Jeannie: (Nervous laughter) Now what?

Brown: (Voice soft, dreamy) Put your hand between your legs.

More silence.

Brown: Is it wet?

Jeannie: (Her voice quiet, kind of thick now) Uh-huh.

Brown: Pretend. Pretend it's me down there. Just move your hand slowly back and forth.

A long silence now with nothing but static air humming over the line. Craig thinking—knowing as he thought it that this would prey on his mind the rest of his life—that he should have gone up there with Barry, or gone in place of him, but it had been a mistake to let him go alone.

Jeannie: What are you doing?

Brown: (An edge to his voice) What do you think I'm doing? Playing poker?

Jeannie: (Breathy) Is it hard?

Brown: Yeah. Pointing right at you. Tell me when you're going to come.

Listening to more static air, Craig tried to imagine what it would be like as a kid, Barry's age, to come home from school and find your father with his face blown away. How was that going to affect you? And then a couple years later your mother dies. Barry had got through it, though, apart from some bad years as a teenager.

There was some heavy breathing going on between Miami and Montreal.

Jeannie: Oh, God.

Brown: (Whispering) Yeah?

Craig didn't want to listen to this part. It wasn't funny or exciting anymore. Brown telling her what he wanted to do to her, directing her like she was an actress in a porn flick. Instead of just two people trying to get together via the phone. Reach out and touch someone. Reach out and clobber someone was more like it. The telephone, it could be a brutal instrument, Craig thought. Although it was the best weapon he had in his arsenal. You spent hours on the telephone lying to people, trying to locate the person you were tracking. It would be impossible to count the number of times he'd offered free stereos to people, or called posing as a lawyer doling out an inheritance. He'd even been a distant relative on occasion, looking for love.

All just to trap someone into revealing information.

It had got so he couldn't even talk on the telephone anymore on a personal or intimate level. He was always digging for information. He looked at the damn thing there on the desk, black and ugly, with its row of push-button numbers, and thought about picking it up and throwing it against the tape recorder. But that wasn't going to slow Brown now.

The girl was moaning and Brown was still whispering to her as they both climaxed. He could play this over and over and it would always be the same. With the same ending. If it were a movie all he'd have to do is cut the tape and splice in a different ending because now he knew how he wanted it to end. But it wasn't a movie, and Craig wasn't a film director any more than Brown was. A mistake was made, and Craig knew he had no way of going back and correcting it.

Brown: (Voice still low-pitched, breathing heavily) How was it?

Jeannie: Jesus. (Pause) When am I going to see you?

Here was where he began paying attention again. Craig took his feet off the desk and leaned forward in his chair, resting his elbows on his knees, the coffee cup dangling from his forefinger.

Brown: Soon. Listen, I'm going to call Frank tomorrow in New York. See if we can't make a different arrangement. It's too goddamned cold up here. I'm not used to this. If I can't get out I'll send for you, bring you up for a week.

Jeannie: Do you think he'll do that, let you come back here? Is it safe?

Brown: I've been up here for a month now. I can sneak back in. Who's going to know?

So do it, Craig thought. If I hadn't found you, you might have been back here, tomorrow, next week. Then it would have been different. With just one minor adjustment to the script it could all have been different. Instead:

Brown: (Whispering again) Somebody's outside in the hall. Listen, I'll call you later.

Craig listened to the two receivers being replaced and then the endless turning of the reel of tape. What happened next he didn't need to have described to him. Brown getting out of bed, reaching for the .45 beneath his pillow, moving quietly to the door. Barry outside the door, maybe making a commotion, trying to get the guy inside to open up, or maybe just nosing around checking things out. Always counting on the element of surprise.

Whatever it was, Brown would have opened the door and Barry would say something like: "I've got a gun; I don't want to use it. Now turn around with your hands behind your back." Barry would have one foot in the door, the cuffs in his hand, maybe even his gun out.

He'd see Brown open the door a little wider, maybe even still naked, his hands behind his back all right, but what he wouldn't see, or might see too late, would be Brown turning away from the door, bringing the .45 up already cocked and ready.

Barry. The thing about Barry, Craig thought, was that he had made himself, invented himself; whatever he was had come from inside him. He had dealt with all the crap he'd been through as a kid and decided he wasn't going to go through life with it hanging around his neck like a stone. Over the years he'd somehow gotten it out of his system. Accepted it. Accepted life for what it was, and was determined to make the most of it.

And to come through all that for what?

To be shot by some half-assed hood on the lam? What was the point?

Craig raised his head, sat up and wiped at his leaky eyes, then switched off the tape recorder.

* * *

Twenty years ago, when Barry was ten years old, tragedy had struck and scarred his young life. Craig, then twenty, recently married, had moved to Miami from New Jersey, where he'd been a cop on the Newark police force. Making a lot of changes.

Finally he was working for himself in a business that had become so demanding in South Florida that people were even coming up with new ways of describing themselves. Bounty hunter was considered a derogatory term now. He was a recovery agent or pickup man. Even a skip tracer. But the way Craig looked at it, what the hell difference did it make what you called yourself? The work was still the same.

Barry had called Craig long distance from New Jersey that day, twenty years ago now, but in his mind it seemed like yesterday. For a while Craig had thought it was a wrong number or a crank call. There was some whimpering on the line, but no one spoke. He was about to hang up when Barry, in a thin voice, said, "Daddy's dead."

Shot in the head with a twelve-gauge shotgun. Barry had found him when he got home from school, lying in a pool of blood on the kitchen floor, most of the right side of his face missing. He'd been dead a couple hours. On any other day Barry's mom would have found him, except this day, when she'd been driving home from her part-time job and had a flat tire.

They never found out who killed him. A string of gambling debts discovered when they went through his papers suggested a motive, even though they couldn't put a face on the killer.

Then a year, year and a half later, Mom died suddenly, leaving Barry an orphan at the age of twelve. He came to live with Craig and his wife. It was like suddenly finding yourself with an adolescent son. The marriage didn't survive, for many reasons, but

Craig knew the final straw came the night he and his wife, Carol, were coming home from a party. Back earlier than they'd planned to the new house in Kendall. They were driving down the street, and as they approached the house they could see something was wrong. The lights were on inside; the curtains to the picture window that opened onto the residential neighborhood were open. As they came closer they could see Barry standing in front of the window. He was naked. Standing in front of the goddamn window naked with all the lights in the house on—holding his cock in his hand. Carol was livid. A week later she was gone, back to New Jersey.

Then it was just Craig and Barry, Barry in his teens, rough going for a while, very rough, Craig wondering whether they could get through it. But they did get through it, and when they did they were brothers again, not the father and son they'd had to become. They were also close. Barry went away to school for a couple of years, and when he came back he went to work for Craig. Barry had his own place but they were together most of the time, drinking, chasing girls, working. They were not only brothers; they were now, also, good friends.

Barry seemed happy. He didn't take life seriously. Living in sneakers, T-shirts, and cutoffs, even making a game out of work. Craig had heard him say more than once, Life's short, so enjoy it.

Yeah, right, Craig thought, as the images of Barry's life reeled across his mind.

It was ten o'clock in the morning before Craig could get through to the assistant prosecutor he wanted in the State Attorney's office. He had listened to the John Brown tape a half dozen times, until he could recite most of the lines before they were spoken. He even had the breathing down. It was a relief when his call finally went through.

"I want some more background on John Brown," Craig said. He had talked personally to the attorney, Les Granger, once, two weeks ago. Granger was in charge of prosecuting Brown. When Brown skipped out on his bail, the bonding agency had called Craig and hired him to bring him back. Craig went to the State Attorney's office and met with Granger. He remembered Granger smoked cigars and a couple of his fingers were bound in gold rings. He got the impression Granger didn't think much of bounty hunters.

"I thought I'd pretty much gone over that," Granger said.

"There are some loose ends," Craig replied.

"Hold on."

Craig waited for the attorney to come back with Brown's file. It was information from the file, the stuff on the girlfriend, Jeannie, that had linked Brown to the apartment in Montreal. Other than the fact that Brown was wanted for murder, Craig didn't know much about the guy; he'd learned more from the tape recording. But his guess was Granger wouldn't cooperate much more, for fear his office could be seen as acting in collusion with bounty hunters.

"What do you want?" Granger asked.

"Who's Frank?" Craig asked. He sensed he'd caught the attorney off guard.

"Frank who?"

"Frank. Brown's friend in New York."

Silence, then Granger asked, "What do you know about him?"

"Brown thinks Frank might let him come back home. Frank seems to control things."

"Frank Bishop," Granger said.

"Who is he?" Craig waited out the next silence.

"Look," Granger said, "there's nothing in this file on Frank Bishop that you or anybody else couldn't find out if you wanted to take the time to dig in the dirt."

"Time's what I don't have right now. Not if you want Brown before Christmas."

"All right," Granger said, "but if anybody asks, you never heard this from me."

"You got my word."

"Frank Bishop lives in New York. He owns a hotel and casino in Atlantic City. He's been involved, probably still is, in drugs. For years he worked for the mob, in the old days running 'storefront' unions for mob-controlled businesses. With the money he made, he invested in Atlantic City before it adopted legal-ized gambling. The feeling is he was trying to do the same thing here in Miami. Buying tracts of land in Dade and Broward County where he could put up casinos if gambling was eventually legalized. John Brown was his front man."

"Brown and Bishop. How far back does that con-nection go?"

"A long way. Brown was always a flunky for Bishop. The boss needed something done, or somebody hit, Brown was there to do it. Underneath the WASP name is a real live mobster."

"So how did he slip away from you?"

"Good question," Granger said. "Blame it on the feds. The thinking is that somebody crossed Bishop on one of his land deals. Bishop got pissed, he's old school, vindictive, and put out a contract on the guy. Brown made the hit, but got caught. We're ready to prosecute on the murder charge, but the feds see a chance to get a bigger fish. They really wanted Bishop. So the feds talk Brown into going into one of their

13

witness-protection programs. They promise him they'll see to it that he gets bond and then protect him through all the pretrial stuff in exchange for his testimony against Frank Bishop. Brown agreed. Nobody bothered to explain to the feds that Brown doesn't keep agreements. Once he got bonded he gave them the slip."

"So the moral of the story is don't trust John Brown."

"Let's put it this way," Granger said. "I wouldn't want the guy standing behind me."

"Thanks for the warning," Craig said. "It comes about twenty-four hours too late."

_____ *Two*

*D*EAR GOD, FRANK BISHOP PRAYED SILENTLY — MORE than forty years ago, at the age of eighteen, he'd actually spent a year in a seminary studying for the priesthood, until someone mentioned to him that sanctity and integrity didn't necessarily go together. He dropped out of the seminary shortly after that, and although he liked explaining to people that his decision not to pursue the priesthood came as the result of that revelation, he knew he would never have become a priest, despite his mother's wishes.

Still, some of the habits died hard, he thought,

watching his son Carl, all 275 pounds of him, pour two containers of cream into his coffee, three packets of sugar, and then reach for his second glazed doughnut of the morning.

Dear God, if I have to have an addiction, and I'm not asking for one, You understand, but if I have to have one, please make it something more interesting than doughnuts.

When he looked in the mirror in the morning he couldn't believe it. Here he was, sixty-one years old and, what, five-seven, five-eight, something like that, but still the same 150 pounds he'd been forty years ago. Except that he really did look priestly now, he thought, bald on top, with thick white hair covering his temples and the back of his head; other than that he still had the looks and energy of a younger man.

So where did Carl, at the age of twenty-one, get this look of a beached whale from? Not his mother, dear God, may she rest in peace, that was for sure. It had to be the fucking doughnuts. Frank wouldn't say anything to Carl of a critical nature, but, Jesus, he'd like to see him drop twenty-five pounds, and eventually get down to two hundred. Otherwise, he was going to be dead in ten years, and what parent wanted to see his child, especially his only son, precede him in death? What was the point of working all these years if he couldn't pass it on to his son?

Assuming there was going to *be* anything to pass on.

"Somebody tried to get to Johnny Brown last night," Frank said. At seven-thirty this morning, as soon as he'd got into the office, Brown had called from Montreal. Frank then called Carl at home. And woke him up. Carl was the nominal president of Bishop Enterprises—even though Frank still made all the decisions—but his son wouldn't show up until nine, sometimes nine-thirty every morning. And go home at five like he was a fucking banker. Frank didn't criticize him about that either, believing it was better to learn by example. But after all these years of coming in at seven and often not leaving before seven in the evening, Frank wasn't sure if Carl had ever even noticed.

Frank watched his son reach for his third doughnut from the Entenmann's box he'd carried in with him. "John Brown? In Montreal?" Carl asked.

"How many other John Browns do you know who would cause me to get you out of bed before eight in the morning?" Maybe it was all that sugar, Frank thought. The boy's brain was going. Or more likely it was just that Carl never got out into the field. The few hours he worked a week were mostly spent in this office.

Frank had bought the building they were in, on West Twelfth between Fifth and Sixth avenues, in 1958. He'd made a bundle operating a jukebox concession in New Jersey, always careful not to have any direct competition with the mob, which seemed to regard the priestly Irishman with grudging respect along with a certain amount of suspicion.

Later Frank set up his own teamsters union and got a lot of the mob business that needed a local for appearance's sake but didn't want anything too rigorous. Frank gave them a "storefront" and everybody was happy. When Atlantic City adopted gambling, Frank got in on the ground floor. The Italians seemed to respect him more. He had always said the only thing their two cultures had in common was a respect for the cloth and a quick temper.

Those early years, Frank was on the road. Taking care of business in New Jersey, and later in New York

17

and Atlantic City. Carl had it easy; he could sit up here in his ivory tower, work from a telephone and a computer—and get fat.

It was time, Frank decided, that his son get his hands dirty. "I want you to go up there," he said.

Carl stopped chewing. A piece of glaze from the doughnut he was eating clung to a corner of his mouth. "To Montreal?"

"To Montreal," Frank said.

"What the hell for?" He whined like a spoiled kid.

"You know as well as I do. They get Johnny Brown back here to stand trial, and we're going to jail."

Carl sipped his coffee. They were sitting in the boardroom at the long, polished table, thick carpeting under their feet, bright pictures on the walls, the central heating controlling the temperature. Frank knew that Carl was taking it all in, worried that he would have to give this up. And he would. It wasn't going to be like this in Montreal.

"We got guys we could send up there," Carl said. "Why me?"

Frank shook his head, looked at his son; the beatific smile that was his trademark in confrontations twisted his thin lips. "Carl, you're my son," he said, paused, then added, "I trust you."

"So what am I supposed to do, sit up there and baby-sit Johnny?"

"Yes," Frank said. "He wants to come back here. You keep him up there until we can figure something out or until the heat's off."

"Jesus, what's it like up there in February?"

"Cold. Lots of snow. Maybe you guys can go cross-country skiing, get a little exercise. It'll be good for you. Think of it as a vacation."

Carl shook his head and said, "I'd rather go south."

Frank ignored the sarcasm. "Do me a favor and call

your sister, see what she's up to." Frank hadn't talked to his daughter in a month. He couldn't figure her out. She was twenty-two and she had problems. A little more than a month ago she'd taken an overdose of Valium. Jesus, Colleen. He was still having a hard time dealing with that. She was working on her master's degree at NYU; as far as he knew, without serious problems. The next thing, her roommate calls to say Colleen's in the hospital. OD'd, is what she said.

"She makes me nervous," Carl said. "What am I supposed to talk to her about?"

Frank thought: she's your sister, talk to her like ordinary people talk to their families. Knowing, though, that there was little love lost between Carl and Colleen. But the fact was, she made Frank nervous too. God, how did families get themselves into these messes?

Frank wished she'd get married, but she never talked about boys. He'd even tried to introduce her to guys he knew. A couple years ago she'd gone out with one of them, a guy who worked for Frank. In the middle of dinner she got up and walked out. Just like that, in the middle of dinner! No explanation. She was too headstrong for her own good. The thing was, Frank wanted grandchildren and he was afraid Colleen was his only hope. He doubted if Carl could find his dick with both hands under all that fat.

"See how she's doing, that's all," Frank said. Colleen had taken this term off. She was going to stay home and read and just take it easy. "I may have something, a project that might interest her."

He watched Carl reach for the last doughnut in the box, the sixth. Dear God, he thought. Where did I go wrong?

*　*　*

Colleen listened to her brother's voice on the phone and wondered what it was about him that her father found so appealing, apart from Carl's being his only son. The answer seemed obvious, one word—subservient. Frank Bishop could control Carl. In fact, the only person in Frank's world he couldn't control was Colleen. And she knew how much that bothered him.

"How are you?" Carl asked.

"I'm just fine," she said. There was a long silence in which she could practically *hear* Carl searching for something else to say. Something that wasn't going to upset her and cause her to yell at him.

"You keeping busy?"

"As busy as I want to keep," she said.

"What about Dad, you talk to him recently?"

"Not in over a month. Why?"

"Give him a call. He's got something that might interest you."

Colleen laughed. "You mean something that interests him. Something he wants me to do for him." It was funny. Because she had an education, Frank seemed to think that whenever he needed some work done that required a brain instead of muscle, Colleen was the person to do it. She was always being asked to write something for him. She was surprised he'd never asked her to write his memoirs. Although on second thought she couldn't imagine him revealing anything about himself except that he'd once been to divinity school.

"Frank tell you to call me?"

"Dad asked me to call you, yes." A strange sibling difference. To her Frank was Frank; to Carl, he was Dad. Of course, they weren't siblings at all, since she was adopted, a fact that she had long ago decided was the reason Frank treated her the way he did.

"So why didn't he call himself?" she asked. She was just making conversation, knowing what he would say. Maybe she just wanted to goad Carl into a confrontation, knowing how he detested confrontations. She got a perverse pleasure from teasing him.

"You know as well as I do." There was irritation in Carl's voice; Frank had probably been riding him.

The truth was she didn't know. It would take a shrink to explain Frank Bishop. She had once humiliated him by walking out on a guy who Frank had set her up with. She hadn't wanted to go out with the guy in the first place. Frank, as usual, was persistent. She relented. The guy bored her. He had a hard time expressing himself except when it came time to proposition her. Which he made the mistake of doing while they were eating. Frank blamed her, like he always did, and never forgave her.

"Yes, of course," Colleen said. "How could I have forgotten? He's busy. He doesn't have time to pick up a phone and dial a number."

Carl sighed. "Colleen, why not just call him and talk to him? Make it easy on both of you."

Easy. Other than the fact that she knew Frank had some connection with unions, some business interests in Atlantic City, probably ties to the mob, and God knows what else—there, she even sounded like Frank —she was never privy to what went on in the day-to-day Bishop business world.

"What about you, Carl? How are you? What are you doing with your life?"

"I'm going to Montreal," he said. As if getting out of New York were his way of showing independence.

"What for?" She really didn't care, but whenever Carl moved out of Frank's sight it could be interesting.

"There's a guy up there I've got to baby-sit."

All her life she'd been around men who were always protecting each other. Businessmen. As a kid her friends had fathers who were doctors or salesmen, something you could identify, know what they did. Frank was just a businessman, and his friends were all businessmen. All very successful. Before her mother died, when she was twelve, Colleen learned to avoid direct questions where Frank was concerned. Later she rejected that lesson.

"Is Frank in trouble?" she asked.

"He could be if the guy in Montreal goes to trial."

"And you'll be there to see that he doesn't," Colleen said. "Some day, Carl, you're going to have to stand on your own two feet. Don't you think it's about time you got up off your knees?"

"C'mon, Collie, please don't give me a hard time."

Colleen laughed. Collie. She hated Carl's nickname for her, had always hated it. "All right, Carl. It can't be easy trying to follow in Frank's footsteps. In the unlikely event something happens to him while you're gone, how do I get in touch with you? Or is that another secret shared only between the male Bishops?"

"Don't talk crazy."

"Why not? You both think I'm crazy, why shouldn't I talk that way?"

Carl sighed again. He gave her his Montreal address and phone number. And said, "What do I tell Dad?"

"Tell him when he wants me to do something, to call and ask me himself."

She hung up thinking Carl didn't have the balls to repeat that to Frank Bishop.

She had a whole term to sit around and do nothing, she thought—or a term to do whatever she wanted, was another way of looking at it. While she was in the

22

hospital recovering, she had at first thought the best thing to do would be to get back into school. Keep busy. But later, as she got to feeling better, she decided she didn't want to do that. She wanted to take some time off.

Her doctor, a young intern with sandy hair that looked like it was filled with static electricity, and freckles covering the backs of his clean, manicured hands, said he thought she had made a good decision.

"Rest," he said. "And take things easy. You're too young for this kind of stress."

Colleen nodded and smiled. She did a lot of that in the hospital. Smiling. When she was alone, sometimes she'd even break out laughing for no apparent reason. The sandy-haired doctor spent a lot of time with her, talking to her, asking her questions about her life at NYU. She told him she was working on her master's.

"Oh, you're writing a thesis then," he said. "What's it on?"

"A literary history of orphans in nineteenth-century American fiction," she said.

"Wow," he said. "I never even knew there were any. Name one." In the intern's expression she could see a freckle-faced kid of ten. Serious, intent. Trying to make the Little League team.

"How about Huck Finn?" she said.

The intern snapped the thumb and middle finger of his right hand. "Of course," he said. And then thoughtfully, "Why did you choose that for a thesis?"

Colleen smiled. She was going to have fun with this. "I was adopted," she said. "I guess that had something to do with it."

"Really," he said. "Tell me about it."

There was nothing to tell. She was adopted when she was a baby. When she was seventeen, eighteen, she'd tried unsuccessfully to find out who her natural

23

John Leslie

parents were. Why did you want to find them? the
intern wanted to know. It's like a mystery, Colleen
told him. You want to solve it. Something in your past
that's been withheld from you, like there's a whole
side to you that you don't know anything about.

"What happened? Why didn't you find them?"

"Frank, my father, wouldn't go along. He's the only
one who knew about it."

"How did you feel about that?"

Colleen shrugged. "Let down, I guess."

"How do you get along with him?"

"I don't see him that much."

"In general," the intern said.

Colleen smiled. "I don't like him," she said.

"Why?"

Colleen tugged at the covers of her bed. Until that
moment she had no idea she was going to tell this guy,
who she kept seeing as a boy rather than a doctor,
things she had never before told anyone. She just
began talking.

About six months after her mother died Frank came
into Colleen's room one night and got into bed with
her. She woke up, sleepily wondering what he was
doing there. He said he couldn't sleep, he'd just stay a
minute. Colleen curled up next to him and fell asleep
again.

This went on periodically for a month. Until one
night she woke up and discovered Frank fondling her.
She remembered laying very still, afraid, unsure what
to do. She was embarrassed, ashamed, guilty, and
frightened all at the same time. Somehow she found
the courage to jump out of bed and, before he could
grab her, run across the room to the bathroom, where
she locked herself in. She spent the rest of the night on
the floor in the bathroom.

After that Frank kept to his own room and neither

of them ever mentioned that night. It was soon afterward that she began calling Frank by name instead of Dad, and her curiosity became aroused about who her real parents were. But Frank was never helpful, and she had nothing to go on.

Eventually, when she got into college, she outgrew her obsessions with her family and just wanted to be left alone.

When she finished talking, the intern said, "I see." Colleen smiled. A week later she was released and went back to her West Village apartment.

Last year she had come into a trust fund that Frank had set up for her which would give her nearly a hundred thousand dollars a year over the next five years. That was to be her share of the family fortune.

Her fat brother, Carl, who was a year younger, was already making a hundred thousand a year salary for doing nothing more than scraping his knees in front of his father. And he would go on to make even more. She didn't complain about the inequity. She could invest well and take care of herself. Carl she wasn't so sure about.

And all of this because Carl was flesh and blood.

So whoever said life was fair?

As she mulled over her future, Colleen decided it would be nice to talk to the one man from her childhood who had never caused her problems. Julius Stearns had always been like a grandfather to her, even though he was only ten years older than Frank. She would avoid telling him about her stay in the hospital. Julius already thought too much about death.

Maybe he would have some suggestions about how she should spend this term, in case she got bored sitting around New York. Of course, she had money;

she could travel. What people with money who had nothing to do but die always did. Around the world in a month, eighty days, whatever it took. Which sounded, when you thought about it, pretty silly. She'd rather write. But a literary history of orphans in nineteenth-century American fiction?

Anyway, she'd already confronted her mortality at the age of twenty-two. There were other things to write. Maybe a personal memoir. She could expose Frank. Something she had dreamed about doing when she was younger. With a little digging, some insider detective work, she could probably single-handedly have put him behind bars. Something no law enforcement agency had ever been able to do.

Julius Stearns was playing checkers with Mrs. Duke on the porch of the Hotel C-Breeze on Ocean Drive. Eighty-five degrees on Miami Beach in the middle of February, as an exuberant voice kept reminding them from a radio inside the residential hotel's lobby while they sat outside on the porch looking across the beach to some palm trees which were turning yellow, beyond to the water which was as calm as a lake. You'd think a man would be happy with this view, Julius thought.

He looked around him at the gang of people sitting in the green and white plastic lawn chairs lined up like sitting ducks in a shooting gallery on the porch. If there were anyone under sixty-five here, he'd be surprised. Most of them were closer to his age, seventy-one, leaning on canes, squinting across the beach, probably barely able to see the water.

Who in hell wanted to stare at water all day anyhow? Julius thought. It was boring. Life was boring. When you got to this age, if you couldn't do anything but sit on a porch all day and play checkers, you might as well walk across the road, down to the beach, and just keep on walking until you got a couple of fathoms of water over your head.

The thing was, Julius could do something else. If he could get a bankroll he was pretty sure he could put together a new life that wouldn't involve beating the pants off Mrs. Duke at checkers every day. The last thing he wanted to see was Mrs. Duke without her pants, so he usually took it easy on her, let her win a few games.

He'd let his mind wander, thinking about a roulette wheel in the Bahamas. He'd work on his system, refining it in his head until he felt that it was second nature to him, while at the same time trying to come up with a scheme that would get him a sufficient bankroll to stake him to a week at the tables, where he was pretty sure he could earn a couple grand a day, depending on the size of his stake.

With that kind of money he could begin living again.

In the meantime Mrs. Duke was jumping and crowning herself to glory and, eventually, victory. "That's two out of three. You're losing your touch, Mr. Stearns," Mrs. Duke said.

"Ain't life a bitch," Julius said.

"Well, if you're going to be a sore loser we don't have to play."

"It's all right, Mrs. Duke," Julius said, laying out the worn red checkers on his side of the board. "I lost my concentration, that's all." What he had, though, was the beginning of an idea for his grubstake. Maybe he'd let Mrs. Duke win another one while he worked on this idea.

"Julius, telephone," Harvey, the day desk man, called from the open window of the hotel.

Julius stood up and walked spryly through the lobby. "Who is it, Harvey?" he asked, looking at his watch.

"Sounds like a young lady," Harvey said.

"Any woman under sixty's a young lady around here. I better take it in my room in case I get excited. I don't want to embarrass anyone."

Julius took the elevator up to the fourth floor and stepped out on the frayed and faded corridor rug and across to his room. When he picked up the receiver he looked at his watch again. It had taken him forty-seven seconds to get there from the porch. Not bad for seventy-one.

"Julius," he said, the way he'd been answering a phone for more than fifty years.

"Hi. It's me. Colleen."

"Yeah, well, what took you so long? I was just thinking about you less than ten minutes ago."

"You were? I was thinking about you then too. I'm not going to school this term. I'm researching a book I want to write."

"Yeah? Well, I'm permanently on a leave of absence and am also thinking about a book. Let's see if we've got the same one in mind, and then we'll know we're cooking. A biography of Meyer Lansky," Julius said.

"Who?"

"I guess we don't have the same project. I want to write a book about Meyer Lansky, the guy I worked for for forty years. Remember?"

"Oh, him."

"Yeah, him. Show some respect. One of the biggest crime figures in America. He started Murder, Inc., but he's dead now so I guess I don't have to worry about getting killed. If it makes you feel any better, though, I'll tell you that when you reach seventy you don't worry much about dying anyway."

"Thanks, Julius. You're so cheerful."

"It comes from playing checkers all day with old ladies. How's Frank?"

"Frank's the same. He doesn't talk to me much."

"You're lucky, but don't worry, it's not like Frank to keep his mouth closed for long. You want to help me write that book or not?"

"I don't know," Colleen said. "Frank also seems to have something he wants me to do."

"I thought he wasn't talking to you?"

"Through Carl."

"He must be a pretty big boy by now."

"Don't make fun. He doesn't like to be teased."

"So you can't help me write this book and make my fortune?"

"I didn't say that. Maybe we can help each other."

"What kind of help do you need?"

"I've been sitting around here today wondering about my real parents."

Julius swallowed. "That again?" he said. "I thought you laid all that to rest awhile back."

"I guess it's the book I'm writing. It's about orphans."

"Great," Julius said. "I can see it now. Orphans and Meyer Lansky by Colleen Bishop. I like it. It's got a certain ring to it."

"I've already got a title. 'A Literary History of Orphans in Nineteenth-Century American Fiction.'"

"Boy, oh, boy," Julius said. "I can see you're not reaching for the best-seller lists. Why don't you come down to Florida, get out of the cold for a while and we'll talk?"

Colleen laughed. "I'll think about it."

"Good. Let me know what you decide so I can move the old lady out of the way for you."

Julius hung up and went back down to the porch.

Mrs. Duke was asleep. It was just as well. He would go down to the Strand, have a Bombay gin on the rocks with three olives, and dinner. See some young people for a change. Think about Meyer Lansky. And figure out what to tell a twenty-two-year-old woman about her parents.

_____ *Three*

A CONTACT IN NEW YORK, A GUY WHO RAN A FULLY staffed recovery agency—one of those who abhorred the term bounty hunter—provided Craig with the information he was looking for twenty-four hours after Craig called from Miami. What he got was better than anything Les Granger had been able, or willing, to give him.

Bishop was up there. He wasn't in a league with the Bonannos, Gambinos, or Genoveses, but the Irishman had no trouble filling a dance card, as the New York agent put it.

There was personal stuff. Bishop lost his wife to cancer in '77. They had two kids, a girl named Colleen, and a boy, Carl. The oldest, the girl, was adopted. Carl was nominal head of Bishop Enterprises, but the old man still ran things. It was the kind of information Craig was after, the sort of stuff he knew he could make use of. The agent even provided him with addresses and phone numbers for the entire family.

What he got on John Brown was equally good, maybe even better.

"He was muscle," the agent said. "Loyal only as long as he was being paid. You heard of the Shah of Iran?"

"Of course," Craig said. Who was likely to forget the guy, the King of Kings? Especially after he was forced to flee, and later his countrymen took nearly a hundred hostages and held them in the American embassy in Teheran.

"The story is, the feds hired Brown to drive the Shah around when he arrived in New York to go to the hospital here. They couldn't risk anybody 'official,' so they hired a hit man from the mafia."

"Jesus," Craig said. "The guy's working both sides of the street."

"Yeah, that wasn't the first time. And it probably won't be the last. Brown's been around, but he owes everything to Frank Bishop."

"Bishop know about Brown's other life?"

"Yeah. It seems like it. And he probably likes it, you know, playing the superpatriot game. But Brown's got a reputation now, and he's trading on it. Apparently he's in some hot water down where you are, a murder rap I hear. Something Bishop set up."

"You've got your ear to the ground, all right," Craig said.

"I also hear he's flown the coop. You after him?"

"Something like that."

"I guess I don't have to tell you to be careful," the agent said.

Craig hung up and spent a couple hours thinking out the best way to handle the information he'd just been given. Then he made a call to Ellen Schumacher, a woman in Kendall he knew who was afflicted with multiple sclerosis and existed on odd jobs and piece-work that she could perform at home, where she was more or less confined. Craig had no need for a full-time secretary. The little work he was able to give her supplemented her monthly Social Security and Medicare checks.

She answered the phone on the first ring. "Ellie, sweetheart, I've got some secretarial work for you," Craig told her.

"Good. It's been getting boring around here lately. I can use some excitement."

"I don't know how much of that you'll get, but you may get some phone calls. I'm resurrecting Connections." Connections was the name for a front operation he'd set up a few years ago. Trying to get a lead on a fugitive, family members would often put Craig, in one of his various poses, on the right trail without even knowing they were doing it. If there were any doubts later and the family decided to check up on Craig by calling the business number he'd given them, they would get Ellen Schumacher.

"Who are you this time?" Ellie asked.

"Craig Simmons. If anyone calls you, a distant relative of a girl who was given up for adoption twenty odd years ago has died and left money to the girl— now a woman. We've been contacted to try and find her."

"What's her name?"

"Colleen Bishop," Craig said.

It took another day to connect with Colleen Bishop. When he finally got through he said, "Miss Bishop, my name is Craig Simmons." He kept his voice low, without animation, the dumb bureaucrat. "I'm with an agency, a private agency, here in Miami, called Connections. We handle a lot of missing persons stuff, runaways, spouses who have disappeared without a trace, even kidnappings once in a while, if the authorities don't seem to be getting anywhere. We've got a hotline. You wouldn't believe it, the number of people who wind up in Florida from across the country."

"Are you looking for money?" Colleen asked. "How did you get my number?" She sounded irritable.

"The other thing we get a lot of," Craig continued, ignoring her questions, "is relatives looking for kids that were given up for adoption years ago." And paused.

"I don't believe this," Colleen said, but her voice was less irritable now.

"Not always parents either," Craig continued. "Sometimes there'll be a death in the family and money to give away. Maybe it's a guilty conscience, I don't know, but often the kid is left an inheritance by the natural family. Twenty, thirty years may go by, but somebody has never forgotten."

"Did Julius get in touch with you?"

"Julius?" Craig asked. This was good, the way it happened. You'd go through a spiel like that and never know what people would say, what kind of useful information they could lay on you. He reached for a pencil.

"Julius Stearns."

He wrote the name on a note pad. "No," Craig said. "I haven't talked to anyone by that name. Who is he?"

"Then what's this all about?"

"Somebody has not forgotten," Craig said, drawing it out, a little emotion in his voice now. And another pause.

"I don't believe it," Colleen said. "This is some crank call. You're putting me on. Who are you working for?"

"This is not a crank call," Craig said. He gave her the name again and Ellie Schumacher's phone number.

"You know I'm adopted. You're saying someone from my . . . family, my real family has left me something?"

"That's exactly what I'm saying."

"Who is it?"

"I can't tell you that. They left the money on the condition that they remain anonymous."

"Then I won't take the money. Just tell me who it is."

Without even asking how much it was. Craig thinking maybe there was more here than he'd anticipated. She was interested—but not in the money. He was on to something. "I can't do that," he said.

"Why not?" Colleen asked.

"Look," Craig said, "I'm coming to New York in a couple of days. I'll need to verify certain things with you personally before I can release the check. Let's get together and talk about this."

"Did you talk to my father, Frank?"

"No," Craig said.

"Then how did you find me?" Suspicion creeping into her voice again.

"That's my job," Craig said, "finding people."

* * *

"It's crap," Frank Bishop said. "There is no money."

"How do you know?" Colleen asked. She had debated whether or not to tell Frank about Craig Simmons's call. In the end she decided it could be worth it. Maybe she would learn something.

"We checked all that stuff out before you were adopted," he said.

Colleen pressed him. "Then you know who my parents are."

Frank sighed. "Dear God," he said. "This is a terrible conversation. Your mother and I raised you as our own. We are your parents."

"Oh, Frank, please don't get sentimental. It doesn't suit you." She didn't want to fight with him. She'd been out of the hospital ten days, relaxed, feeling pretty good about herself, when this guy Simmons calls from Miami. She'd been going to therapy regularly, and she wasn't worried about the suicide thing anymore. It wasn't going to happen again—a stupid thing to do. Because of stress, because of anxiety. Because she'd had such a fucked-up childhood. But it was over now and she was in control. She said to Frank, "You made your choice years ago."

"Why are you saying these things?"

"Think about it, Frank."

"I don't know what you mean."

"You mean you don't want to know. Because you don't want to remember how you treated me."

"That's enough," Frank said. His voice quiet, trembling, and she realized she might have pushed him too far. "I want to know who this guy is, Colleen. I want to know all about him. He's stirred something up for some reason and I want to know why. He comes to New York or calls you again, I want to talk to him."

"I'll give him your number. Julius wants me to come down to Florida to see him."

"What the hell for?"

"He wants to write a book. He thinks I can help him."

"For the love of God, a book about what?"

"Meyer Lansky."

"Meyer? Meyer's dead. You want to know about Meyer, talk to me. I'll tell you plenty about Meyer Lansky. What does a bookkeeper like Julius Stearns know?"

"He was Meyer's bookkeeper," Colleen reminded him.

"Listen," Frank said. "Why don't you ever call me? Talk to me? Maybe I've got some things you could do for me. But no, you're too stubborn. You'll go all the way to Florida to talk about a book with Julius. You won't even come downtown to help me."

"Do you want to appeal to family loyalty, Frank?"

"Call it whatever you want. I'm just trying to help you."

"Then tell me who my real parents were."

"Dear God, where will this end?"

"You tell me, Frank."

"Listen," he said. She knew he was going to change the subject now. He couldn't deal with this kind of stuff. "If you want to go to Florida, maybe I can get you down there and you can do something for me at the same time."

"Is this what you wanted? Why you had Carl call me?"

"Carl's your brother. You ought to talk to him more often."

"We speak different languages," Colleen said.

Frank sighed. She saw where Carl picked that up. "You want to hear about this, or not?"

37

"Of course," Colleen said.

"I've got a guy who's taking a group of people down there on a bus. You want to ride along, you can keep your eye on things. Tell me how it goes."

"Is there going to be trouble?"

"Dear God," Frank said. And sighed again. "I hope not."

Frank felt sorry for her. As a father he guessed he had failed her. He prayed that when she got older she could find it in her heart to forgive him. He also prayed that she got older. The way things were going, that was no foregone conclusion. If her mother had only lived, Colleen might have had a better chance. Frank wasn't good with girls, that was clear. He was used to being in control, dealing with men, and didn't know when to let up. He had never apologized to anyone in his life. He thought it would be a sign of weakness. He was getting old; he needed all the strength he could muster right now.

Which was one reason Sylvester Gallanti's proposal had appealed to him. Sly had walked into his office, what was it, six, maybe eight weeks ago? Talk about old! The guy was over seventy, had been out of prison three months after being inside twenty years for murder. The feds had nabbed him, thinking they could get him to turn on the Gambino family, who he'd been working for. But Sly kept his mouth shut and did his time, all of it. Paid his debt to society. And here he was, looking to go to work.

He came into Frank's office a couple months ago, shook hands, made small talk, and when Frank showed him into the boardroom, Sly dug some photos out of his coat pocket and handed them to Frank.

Frank looked at the color pictures, before and after, of an old Continental Trailways coach that had been customized inside and out. He played along, made the right sounds as he looked at the pictures, and then handed them back to the grinning Sly Gallanti. "What is it?" Frank asked.

Sly stopped grinning. "What d'ya mean what is it? It's a fuckin' bus."

"I can see that," Frank said. "But it's more than that. You got a reason for showing me the pictures."

Sly grinned again. "Yeah, it's more than that, all right. I heard about this guy in Tennessee when I was inside who fixed up old buses and sold them. When I got out I went down to see him, bought this one and had him custom fit it the way I wanted it."

"Must have cost some money."

"Damn near everything I had," Sly said. "About a hundred grand. Money I'd invested before I went inside that had nothing to do but earn interest for twenty years."

"And you blew it on a bus."

"Another investment," Sly said. "I'm going to run some trips to Florida, take the elderly down there, give them a vacation."

Frank stared at him. He could tell Sly was stringing this out; he had something for Frank but he was going to take his time getting to it. Frank played along. "Hell of a slow return on your investment, isn't it?"

Sly grinned again. "It's a round trip. I got to bring those people back from Florida."

Frank couldn't be sure where Sly was going with this. "That pays more than taking them down there?"

"Yeah, you see it, don't you? A few extra suitcases piled in with all those old people's bags? And who's going to look at them, you know what I mean?"

"Yeah, but why are you telling me?"

"I'm a felon. I need a backer, someone who can get the licenses I need from the ICC people. That kind of thing. Also some seed money. I'm broke. But I got a driver and some contacts in Florida. The thing's a cinch, a gold mine. Who's going to bust a bus with a buncha old folks making maybe their last trip to Disney World?"

Frank wondered. He had lost his shirt a few times in moving product, but when it went right, the profit margin was as wide as the Hudson River. The thing was to find more ingenious ways to move it. Sly had something original. "Give me the details," Frank said.

Sly did, and two months later they were in business.

Four

_S_INCE SHE'D COME OUT OF THE HOSPITAL COLLEEN BISH-
op found herself paying more attention to people. She
watched them, observed little things about them that
ordinarily she wouldn't have noticed. Sometimes she
even made up stuff based on what she saw.

With Craig Simmons, however, she just watched.
Closely.

He was implike, with curly blond hair, and a boyish
face despite the cold look in his blue eyes. He reminded her of a cop, the stern, withheld expression in
the ageless face. He might be thirty, he might be forty;

it was hard to tell, she thought. He was questioning, probing, like a doctor embarrassed by the familiarity necessary to examine a patient. Still, she mistrusted him the way she generally mistrusted doctors and cops. Not because of what they were, but *who* they were. Men. She had learned that much growing up around Frank Bishop: that men were not to be trusted.

She sat facing Craig Simmons in a red vinyl booth of the coffee shop on Charles Street, not far from her apartment. At three o'clock in the afternoon the place was not busy, a few coffee drinkers sitting at the counter, a couple of other booths taken with people having a late lunch. Craig sat stirring his coffee, still wearing his car coat with its fleecy zip-in liner that she noticed when he had unbuttoned it to sit down.

"This is pretty funny," Colleen said.

"What's funny about it?" Craig asked.

"You calling me the other day out of the blue. I'm writing about orphans."

"One of those coincidences. Like you'll be thinking about someone you haven't seen in a long time, and a few hours later they call you on the phone or you run into them on the street. That ever happen to you?"

"Sometimes," Colleen said. "But this seems different."

"Not really. More time has gone by, that's all."

What was it about him? On the surface he seemed relaxed, easygoing, the sort of person you could have coffee with every day and let your hair down, talk about anything, and he would nod and understand without being judgmental or critical. On the surface. Beneath the surface there seemed to be a lot of tension. She wondered if Frank could be right. Was Simmons trying to stir something up?

As if reading her mind, he said, "Did you tell your father I talked to you?"

"Yes," she replied.

"What did he say?"

She smiled. "That it's crap. His words."

"That often happens. Which is why I contacted you first instead of him, but I'll want to talk to your father—Frank, right?"

"Frank wants to talk to you too," she said.

"What does he do?"

Colleen laughed. "Frank always describes himself as a businessman. I guess he does what all businessmen do. He makes money."

"And you have a brother too, don't you? Carl?"

"You want to talk to him?"

"It helps to meet with everybody in the family."

Now he sounded like an undertaker. Solicitous, comforting the family.

"Carl's in Canada," Colleen said.

"Canada? He live up there?"

"No," Colleen said. She heard the note of surprise in his voice. "He's there on business." She was getting a sense of something now. Deciding it was time for caution.

"Some of this stuff can be embarrassing."

"In what way?"

"People have pasts. You know, you get a couple, maybe they've got a record. They have a kid they can't afford to take care of so they give it up for adoption. The kid winds up in a better home and the new parents don't want any reminders of where he came from."

"Is that my situation?" Colleen asked. Simmons jumped around a lot. She'd begin to have an idea where he was going, and then he'd be off on a different tack. The thing was, she wanted to believe him.

"You're different," he said. "Somebody had some money, or came into it, and decided they owed you

43

something. As I said on the phone the other day, maybe they had a guilty conscience, I don't know."

"And you won't tell me who it was?"

"I can't. It's part of the deal."

Now convinced that he was lying. But going with it, seeing where he would lead her. "Suppose I'm determined. If you won't tell me, how do I find out?"

He shrugged. "Agencies won't help much without the family's permission. You could hire somebody, I suppose, to dig around."

"Someone like you?"

"Maybe," he said. "I don't know how far they'd get. You mentioned Julius Stearns the other day. Who is he?"

"An old family friend. Someone Frank's age. I told him what I wanted to do." He was digging information from her; she knew it, but it was that surface friendliness, his effortless, disconnected questions that made it easy to talk to him. Maybe she should just clam up, stop talking.

"Family friends can sometimes be helpful," he said. "Talk to him. And I'll tell you what. When I get back to Miami I'll see what I can do for you."

"Thanks."

A waitress came with a Pyrex coffeepot. Simmons put his hand over his cup. Colleen shook her head. "Will there be anything else?" the waitress asked.

"I guess not," Colleen said. The waitress left the check and walked away. "Is that it, then?"

"I think so," Simmons said, standing up to button his coat. "Oh," he paused, reaching for the check— and then smooth, like he'd almost forgotten something—"you were going tell me where I can reach your brother Carl."

"Was I?" Standing up to face him, motionless by the booth. It was all clear to her now where this had been leading, like suddenly seeing the end of a puzzle. She smiled. "Perhaps you should ask Frank," she said.

He had been unprepared for her. As they went out the door of the diner he put his hand on her arm, lightly gripping her just above the elbow. "If you've got another few minutes," he said, "I'd like to walk with you." They stood outside in the cold, the pedestrians walking up Seventh Avenue jostling them.

She looked right at him. "I'm not sure we've got anything left to talk about," she said.

She had seen through his pose; he understood that. He had watched her inside; the mistrust, suspicion, showing in her face as he, lying, had tried to convince her of his sincerity. At one point he thought he had won her over, but in the end, because of the directness with which he had to approach her, he had failed. She was smart, but he had learned two things about Colleen Bishop: she had been deeply hurt at some time in her life, and she did not have much love for Frank Bishop.

Which was why, he decided, there still might be some hope for turning this thing around. Lying, deception, were as much a part of this business as breathing. He had seldom had use for the truth. Until now.

"I want to tell you something," he said. "It won't take long."

He began to tell her about Barry while they walked. They turned off Seventh Avenue to get away from the crowds. The February wind cut through the thin fabric of his car coat and seemed to prick his skin like the cold point of a tattoo artist's needle. He kept his hands plunged deep in his coat pockets and the collar turned up around his ears.

45

She was small. Walking beside him, the top of her head didn't even reach his shoulder. Sitting down she hadn't seemed so small, compact. He was aware of her, her beauty. She'd been sitting in there in a black ribbed sweater that had a roll neck. The sweater wasn't tight, but tight enough to see that she was well-built. Stacked, Barry would say. She had short, tousled, streaked-blond hair that she ran slender fingers through. Her eyes were dark, bright, above a straight nose, full lips, and the hint of a dimpled chin. She was twenty-two but could pass for eighteen. But she wasn't a plaything. And there was a sadness about her that didn't go with her age.

She wasn't Barry's type, but Craig liked her, wished he wasn't working.

He told her everything, stuff about Barry and his life that he'd never talked about before, let alone to a stranger; but in a way, it seemed easier. She walked beside him, her head down, saying nothing. He described the gruesome part of Barry's childhood matter-of-factly. He wasn't trying to create an effect. He just wanted her to know everything. He told her how raising Barry had been like adopting a kid with serious problems, how it had wrecked his own marriage, but how satisfying it was when Barry came through it intact. He told her what he did for a living—Chappell Bros. Security, Inc.—his real name, and how he and Barry had worked together. Then he stopped.

They walked in silence for a while.

Finally she asked the question he had been leading her toward, willing her to ask. "What happened?"

Craig shrugged deeper into the coat, kept walking,

staring straight ahead. "About three weeks ago Barry went to Canada. He was shot."

Colleen stopped, took hold of his arm now. They stood there looking at one another, shivering. "Barry was a good guy," he said. "Not perfect, but good. It was a bullshit thing to happen."

"And you want to find out who did it?"

"Not find out. Find him. I know who did it."

"And you think I can help you?"

"I know you can."

"By going against Frank and my brother?"

"I'm not interested in Frank or Carl or what they've done. I'm not after them."

She didn't say anything, just stood there looking at him, as if she were trying to make up her mind about him again. "I'll sleep on it," she said. "Where are you staying?"

He told her. Then she turned and walked away.

Craig caught a cab back to his hotel, knowing he'd done all he could do. If Colleen didn't come through, he'd have to talk to Frank Bishop. He prayed Colleen had nice dreams about him.

She called the next morning. "I believe you," she said. "But no matter what I think of my brother, I don't want anything to happen to him."

"I told you yesterday. I'm not interested in your brother except to find someone else. I won't hurt him."

There was silence. He could hear her breathing, and pictured the rise and fall of her chest. He waited. Then she told him. The address. The telephone number.

"What does Carl look like?"

"Three hundred pounds of baby fat. You can't miss

him. You could roll him in the snow and have a perfect snowman."

"I hope everything works out for you," he said. And hung up. He wondered why he said that. It seemed like a stupid thing to say. Like he never expected to see her again.

Five

JOHN BROWN SAT ON THE BED IN HIS LONG JOHNS, HIS back against the headboard. Looking out the double window he could watch the snow falling. Looking through the open door he could see shotgun fashion into the kitchen, across the dining room, down a hallway to the open doorway of the front bedroom. It had been snowing for days, the temperature hanging just below the freezing point while Hydro Quebec pumped dry heat from the floor heaters through the thick-walled, double-doored, double-windowed house.

Brown craved moisture, the humidity of the tropics. He dreamed about it, among other things. He sat on a bed littered with newspapers and magazines. He'd never read so much in his life. He hadn't been out of the house in a week, other than to stand on the back balcony in the snow. He hadn't talked to Jeannie in more than two weeks; the phone was now off limits to him. He felt like he was in prison, or back in the army, and he was beginning to have some of the same feelings he had then; he thought he was going stir crazy, and he blamed the fat boy in the bedroom at the other end of the house.

The phone rang. Brown picked up the .45 that lay on the bed buried under newspapers. He watched Carl Bishop lumber from the front bedroom into the hall and answer it. Brown raised the .45, a silencer attached, and aimed it, putting Fat Boy's head in the V of the back sight, holding it there while Bishop held the phone and listened to whoever was on the other end.

When he hung up, Brown watched through the sights as Carl waddled into the dining room, through the kitchen, and into Brown's room, where he stood in the doorway, staring at the barrel of the .45 pointed at him. "Put that thing down," Carl said. "What the hell are you trying to do?"

"Create a little excitement around here." Brown grinned.

Carl ignored him. "That was Frank on the phone."

Brown lowered the revolver and opened the chamber. "Yeah? He give you your instructions for the day? Tell you when to go potty." Brown removed the six bullets from the chamber and lay them in a row on the bed.

"Shut up! Frank's trying to work something out to

get the charges against you dropped. He thinks it may be working."

"What's happening, he getting nervous? Afraid I'll make a break for it, go back to the States and spill what I know about him?"

"He doesn't get nervous."

"What about you, Carl? Do you get nervous?"

"I get tired of listening to you," Carl said. "I don't want to be up here any more than you do. Let's make the best of it."

"But Frank sent you up here, right? To make sure I didn't do anything crazy. Like try to get out of here. What were you supposed to do if I ran, Carl? Kill me?"

"You are crazy," Carl said. "Frank tried to make things easier for you. He wanted you to have some company, and some protection in case anything else happened."

Brown laughed. "Frank must be losing his grip, sending you to protect me." He picked up one bullet and placed it in the chamber of the .45. "And I'll tell you the only company I want, Carl, is female company. This place is beginning to bore the piss out of me. All I do is fucking read."

"Maybe it'll be good for you, give you some education."

"Is that what you think it is, Carl? Education? I'll tell you the education I'm getting. I'm reading the newspaper the other day about a woman who was found dead inside a hollow piece of furniture in a hotel room. She'd been strangled and left in this wooden luggage rack for eight goddamn days. Meanwhile people are checking in and out of the room and nobody finds her. Finally, after eight days, employees discover her after getting a whiff of an unpleasant

51

odor. That's what they say: an unpleasant odor. Now what I want to know, Carl, is what those people staying in that room thought they were smelling if after eight days an employee thought it was an unpleasant odor? Maybe they thought it was just a new air freshener the hotel was trying out."

"That's not funny," Carl said.

"Maybe you'll like this one better. Two buddies are sitting around the house drinking and get into an argument. One of the guys goes out, gets his .357 Magnum, puts a single bullet in the chamber and hands it to his buddy, telling him: 'I'll show you who's got guts.' He then challenged his buddy to put the gun to his head and pull the trigger, saying he would do it next. His buddy took him up on it and shot himself in the head."

"You've got a morbid sense of humor, Johnny."

"But you see, you learn something from this stuff. What if the buddy hadn't shot himself, but pulled the trigger on an empty chamber? Then the other guy's got to do it and he's cut his odds down, don't you see?" Brown eared the hammer back slightly on the .45 and spun the cylinder.

"You're fucking crazy," Carl said.

"Am I?" Brown put the gun to his temple.

"No, no, no. No. You crazy son of a bitch!" Carl shouted.

Brown stared at him, a silly grin on his face, and pulled the trigger. Click. The hammer fell against an empty chamber.

Carl stood in the doorway, his hands over his eyes, sobbing like a goddamn baby. Brown sat there in the center of the bed, like a little boy, cross-legged, still holding the gun, its barrel resting against one long-john-clad thigh.

"Your turn," Brown said.

Carl slowly took his hands from his face, his body still quivering, and looked at Brown, a look frozen with fear. "No," he whimpered. "You're crazy. I'm not playing."

"Look," Brown said. "I'll even give you the same odds I had." He spun the cylinder again.

Carl started to back into the kitchen.

"What's the matter?" Brown asked. "You go out in the fucking snow and slip on the ice, fall under a fucking car, you could be dead." He got off the bed.

Carl was standing in the middle of the kitchen, his arms wrapped around himself like he'd been straitjacketed.

"I start pulling this trigger, you'd be dead, no choice," Brown said. "All you got to do is pull it once and maybe you'll live."

"Leave me alone," Carl said.

Brown walked up to him and cocked the gun in his ear. Carl closed his eyes. Brown put the barrel against Carl's temple. Carl began trembling, hugging himself. "Don't do it," he said. "Please don't do it."

"What is it, fat boy? You afraid to die?"

"Frank had some other news."

"What other news?"

"Don't shoot me?"

"I'm not playing *Let's Make a Deal,*" Brown said. "What else did Frank say?"

"He thinks somebody else may be coming here looking for you."

"Who?"

"He didn't know."

"You making this up, fat boy?"

"No, Johnny, I'm not. That's what he said. We're supposed to be on guard."

Brown lifted the gun away from Carl's temple. Carl kept his eyes closed. His hair was damp with sweat.

53

Brown pointed the .45 through the door into the dining room and pulled the trigger. The gun spat and bucked in his hand when it went off, the bullet tearing a hole in the dining room wall.

Carl began to stomp on the floor like a kid and sob. "Jesus Christ! Jesus Christ! Why did you do that?"

"I guess I'm getting a little edgy, cooped up in here with you," Brown said. "Look at it this way. The one that was meant for you missed. Maybe you'll live a long time."

"You really are crazy," Carl said, still sobbing.

"But not crazy enough to sit around here and be bushwhacked by another bozo trying to take me."

"What are you going to do?" Carl asked, wiping his face, his legs still trembling.

Brown grinned. "I'll tell you what I'm going to do. I'm going to go out and find a woman. I get some pussy, maybe that'll take a little of the edge off. Then I'll figure out what to do."

Carl looked like he was going to start crying again. "Frank doesn't want you going out of here," he whimpered.

"Well, Frank ain't here to know what I do, is he?"

"Johnny, I'll go and bring a girl back here."

Brown looked at him, thinking about all that snow he would have to trek through, getting cold and wet. "Now you're beginning to think. I'm glad I didn't shoot you."

When Carl had on his camel-hair overcoat, ready to go out, he stopped at the door. "Tell me something, Johnny. You were just playing around back there, weren't you?"

Brown grinned at him. "You want to watch your step," he said.

* * *

Craig Chappell met with the MUC homicide detective, who took him over to the morgue where they were keeping Barry's body. An attendant found the right slot, pulled the drawer out and opened the body bag so that Craig could take a look, make sure it was his brother. He stared down at Barry's cold, pale flesh, and stepped back. They returned to the MUC office, where the detective gave Craig another bag, containing Barry's personal effects, including his .38 Smith & Wesson. Craig sat in the office and filled out the forms to get Barry back into the States. Then he phoned to book Barry on a flight to Miami.

"What about John Brown?" the detective asked. Nonchalant, keeping it low-key all the way.

"I don't know," Craig said. "I guess you guys didn't have any luck tracing him?"

The detective shook his head. "Are you still pursuing Brown?"

Craig also shook his head, playing the same low-key game. "The guy's vanished. What can I do?"

The detective nodded. "So you'll take your brother back?"

Craig smiled. "I thought I might take a day or two and look around the town. Get a taste of winter so I can feel better about Miami."

"You think it'll take that long?"

"You never know with these things," Craig said. "But believe me, I'll know when it's time to go."

Christ, he didn't need ten minutes in this place to feel better about Miami. Two feet of snow blanketed Montreal and the stuff was still falling. Who would choose to live in a climate like this? Craig wondered, walking to the parking garage where he'd left his rental car.

55

Tracked plows worked the sidewalks, pushing the snow to curb sides, while larger plows, followed by heavy equipment for shoveling the white compacted powder into dump trucks, worked the streets; the entire parade surrounded by whistles, sirens, bleeps, the scrape of steel against concrete, and flashing lights.

When his car was brought down, Craig took his map of Montreal from the glove compartment and carried it over to the cashier's counter. He took out the address Colleen Bishop had given him and asked the cashier to show him how to get there.

Five minutes later he was skirting the southwestern edge of Parc Mount Royal on the Avenue des Pins. He took Park Avenue to Mount Royal, where he turned right and then the first left on Rue Jeanne Mance. He found 4588 fifty yards down on the left.

The street was chaos.

The snow-clearing equipment had yet to find its way to this narrow street. Most of the cars parked on either side of the one-way street had been shoveled free of snow and were parked at a forty-five-degree angle to the curb to prevent them from being buried in the wake of future plows.

Craig looked at his watch; it was after two-thirty. Another hour and it would be dark up here. He drove around the block, coming back onto Jeanne Mance, finding a parking place several doors down from 4588 on the same side of the street. He backed in against the curb at the same angle as everyone else. From here he could see the front of the house without being seen by anyone inside.

They were row houses, two or three stories, brick or stone construction, with small yards surrounded by iron fences. Craig got out of the car, locked it and walked down the street. Most of the walkways inside the yards were swept clean, he noticed, but not 4588.

Someone had beaten a path to the door by tramping through the snow. A couple feet of snow were on either side of the footpath.

There was a light on in an upstairs window. Craig walked to the end of the block, turned down an access alley, and then another one that paralleled Jeanne Mance from the rear. Here there were garages, balconies on the backs of the houses, clotheslines on pulleys strung from balconies to a tree to another part of the house. Doors gave out onto the alley from the enclosures. Walking along the alley toward his car, it was impossible to tell which house was 4588. It would also be impossible to keep track of both the front of the house and the back alley.

He went back to the car and got inside, started it and turned the heat on high. At least he knew someone had been going in and out of the front, where he chose to begin his surveillance.

Craig got out the thermos of coffee he'd brought along with some cheese and crackers and settled back in the seat.

Two hours later, in the dark, he watched as a fat man in a camel-hair overcoat lead a young woman in a fur-collared leather coat and high boots down the street past Craig's car and into the courtyard at 4588. The guy looked like he was walking on eggs as he tried to keep his feet under him on the icy pavement.

The young woman looked bored.

_____ ***Six***

*T*HE PLAN WAS THAT SHE'D TAKE THE BUS DOWN AS FAR AS Miami, get off, spend some time with Julius, fool around, do whatever she wanted, and then fly back to New York. Frank didn't want her riding the bus when it returned to New York in a couple of weeks. He had been pretty clear that it was to be a one-way ride only, which immediately made her suspicious.

"Why?" she asked him on the phone.

"Why what?" Frank said, like he didn't know what she was talking about.

"You don't want me to come back with the bus."

"I thought you wanted to see Julius." Frank was indignant. "You're supposed to be relaxing, taking a vacation. When you get ready to come back, you can fly. I'll pay for your ticket."

"Payment for spying on a friend of yours."

"You're not spying," he said, growing more exasperated. "Sly's not even a friend. A guy I've known over the years, that's all. We've got a business deal working. I've put some money up and I want to make sure it's a sound investment."

"Bus tours to Florida?" She couldn't believe it.

"There's money in it," Frank said.

Colleen didn't believe him. "Where?" she asked. "It sounds too legitimate."

Frank went into a coughing fit, not even bothering to put his hand over the mouthpiece of the phone. She knew it was an act. When he stopped he said, "You're a radical. Thank God you're young. Maybe you'll grow out of it. I don't know where I went wrong."

"Sure you do."

Frank wheezed and ignored her remark. "You ever hear from that guy again, the one who called wanting to give away money?"

"He came and saw me."

There was a pause before Frank said quietly, "I thought he was going to talk to me."

"I told him. What did you want me to do, lead him down to your office by the hand?"

"What did he want?"

"Nothing."

"What do you mean, nothing?" Frank was shouting now. "The guy calls you with some cock and bull story about an inheritance and you tell me he doesn't want anything."

"He made a mistake," Colleen said. "He had the wrong person."

"What am I supposed to be?" Frank asked. "Dumb? The guy calls you, comes to see you, then says, sorry, he's got the wrong woman. Come on, Colleen. This is me, your father, you're talking to."

"Let's just drop it, Frank. I'll never see him again."

"He pump you for information about me?"

"Of course, Frank. Everybody wants to know about Frank Bishop. Including me."

"Dear God." Frank sighed.

She liked Sly Gallanti. He wore a double-breasted suit with a pocket scarf neatly folded in the breast pocket and used a walking stick on the street. On the bus he talked with the passengers, mostly older people, all unmarried, making their first trip to Florida. A good mix of men and women, and except for Colleen and one guy who was maybe fifty, nobody else was under sixty. SLY'S SINGLES painted on the outside of the bus. A couple weeks of forced companionship, who knows what will happen? Sly said.

He had proudly showed her around the customized interior before the other passengers got on. Smoked glass in all the windows; the seats extra large and deep cushioned; a sound system individually controlled; an area in back where four people could sit around a card table. There was the standard rest room in the back, and a coffee maker and refrigerator containing cold refreshments.

A safe was bolted under a settee directly behind the driver, where valuables could be checked. She saw a handgun mounted on the plywood partition in front of the safe. "You never know," Sly said.

He sat with her when he wasn't playing cupid. She had a seat up front across the aisle from Everett, the black driver, who would sometimes turn the sound system on and croon old-timey stuff in a voice that sounded a lot like Joe Williams. Even live entertainment.

"How did you come up with this idea?" Colleen asked Sly as they rolled along I-95 across Delaware.

"A brainstorm," Sly said. "I had twenty years to work out the wrinkles." He winked.

Colleen studied him, the pallor, the way the skin kind of went slack on his face, like the muscles there hadn't been used that much.

"Frank didn't tell you?" Sly asked, waiting, watching her look him over.

"Jail?" He nodded. "Frank doesn't tell me much about his business."

"Twenty years a ward of the state of New York, and I did it standing up, as they say."

She wanted to ask him about it, what he'd done, but she didn't know if she should. Instead she asked him how long he'd known Frank.

"I don't know him," Sly said. "I know of him. He's been around awhile too. I thought he might be interested in going in on this thing with me. I put everything I had into the bus. I needed a backer."

"I was surprised when Frank told me he was getting into this. Tours. It doesn't sound like Frank. What will it take, five or ten years to get your investment back?"

Sly smiled. "Nothing like that."

Colleen smoothed her skirt over her legs. "I was afraid of that," she said.

They stayed on I-95 except to make scheduled stops at places of historical interest, then stopped at one of the chains, usually Days Inn, at night. Down through Maryland, Virginia, and into North Carolina. "There's more history right on this bus than anything you're going to get looking in an old house, or reading some marker put up alongside the road," Sly said.

"You start talking to some of these people, you'll see what I mean. But they like to have their pictures taken in front of a monument. Gives them the feeling they learned something new."

"What about your history?" Colleen asked.

"Colleen, you're just dying to know why I was a ward of the state for twenty years, aren't you? I been wondering when you were going to ask. I killed a man."

"Why?"

"Why did I kill him? Because I was told to. I got paid to do what I was told."

"And you did twenty years because you wouldn't tell who the man was who paid you."

Sly looked at her, looked at her eyes. "I like living," he said. "So I kept my mouth shut and did my time. Here I am, old, but all in one piece. And you're smarter than I thought."

"I can keep my mouth shut too," Colleen said. "What are you bringing back from Florida that's going to make this trip so profitable?"

Sly stared at her, then clasped his hands. "I got to go see about my paying passengers," he said.

In South Carolina and Georgia she began to feel like she was in the South. The real South, not that gentrified stuff in Virginia. The weather began to improve. It was still wintry gray, but not as cold. They crossed into Florida, and after stopping at St. Augustine, the clouds disappeared and the sun jumped out at them in a blue sky.

They spent the night near Cape Canaveral and the Kennedy Space Center.

The next morning Sly came down the aisle and said to her, "The young guy . . . the one on here under sixty?"

Colleen looked around. The guy was sitting with one of the older women. Colleen had talked to him a couple of times. He made her uncomfortable; she found him too nice, too charming. "He's not young," she said. "Forty-five at the youngest."

"He's a gigolo," Sly said. "A professional. Probably does this all the time."

Colleen laughed. "He's putting the make on the old ladies?"

"More than that. He'll have them signing over their hundred and sixty acre farm in Pennsylvania, if he can find a lady who has one."

"You're going to let him get away with it?"

"I'm quietly having a word with the girls," Sly said, winking again. He moved forward to talk to Everett. Colleen listened as they discussed the remainder of the trip. Everett seemed nervous.

"I tell you I don't like them bridges," Everett said. "I never liked driving them bridges."

"Everett, when was the last time you drove to Key West?" Sly asked.

"Shit. I drove Greyhounds down there for seven years."

"And made your last run when?"

"Ten years ago. Seventy-five, -six, something like that . . . you know that."

"They built new bridges since then," Sly said.

Everett looked at Gallanti like he was crazy. "Well, do tell," he said.

"They got a whole new network now. I read all about it. If you remember, I had a lot of time to read."

"Even that Seven-Mile?"

"A new bridge. Two lane, but four cars could pass if they had to."

Everett shook his head in wonder. "Key West. How come you get a notion to go all the way down there?"

63

"Everett, you think all there is to Florida is Disney World?"

"They got wide roads up here."

"You won't have any trouble with the bridges," Sly said. "Trust me."

Sly turned back to Colleen and grinned. "Everett likes to play it safe."

"I get the feeling you've known him awhile," Colleen said.

"Yeah, I saw him day and night for three years. The difference between murder and robbery. I guess we got to know each other pretty good."

"I think I'll go to Key West with you. I might as well see it all."

"Frank said you'd be staying in Miami."

"I'll stop there on the way back."

Sly shrugged. "I don't see any problem. I'll call Frank and clear it with him."

"I'm twenty-two," Colleen said. "And I don't work for Frank."

Sly smiled and winked. "I don't either."

She was having fun. She chatted with the old people and forgot her own problems. She relaxed. Sly was a riot. He might have killed a man twenty years ago, but for some reason it didn't bother her. She didn't think of him as dangerous. He was smart; he lived by his wits, but he wasn't going to hurt anyone voluntarily. Frank Bishop was a tyrant; Sly Gallanti was a gentleman. Though she was sure there was something illegal in this adventure, she was convinced Sly had values that he wouldn't compromise. She couldn't imagine him taking crap from anyone either. She bet he'd even stand up to Frank if he had to.

They bypassed Miami. Hit that on the way back

from the Keys, along with Disney World, Sly said. She could stay in Miami and visit Julius. And probably never find out what fast-money scheme Sly had going.

They stopped at a Burger King in Homestead for lunch. A couple hours later they were in the Keys, crossing the bridges, the water sparkling like jewels in the sunlight.

At four-thirty they were an hour out of Key West, coming onto the Seven-Mile Bridge, Everett cruising, singing: "Take me home . . . to West Virginia. Take me home . . . country roads."

Sly standing beside Everett, looking out the window, surrounded by water; Colleen leaning forward in her seat as Everett pointed out the narrow old swing bridge that ran parallel with them, the one that had given him nightmares driving for Greyhound. The new Seven-Mile was constructed with a gradual rise toward its center, allowing high-masted sailboats to pass under without holding up traffic on the bridge.

"Didn't I tell you?" Sly said. "Life's a breeze in the Florida Keys."

And then panic. Someone shouted: "Everybody stay in their seats. This is a holdup."

Colleen looked around. The young guy, the gigolo, was moving forward down the aisle, waving a gun. He stopped beside her seat and stood sideways in the aisle covering the passengers and Sly, who was still standing beside Everett.

"Pass the hat. I want everything. Jewelry, wallets, money. Pops," the guy turned to Sly, "get that safe open."

Everett said, "I know'd this was too good to be true."

"Shut up and keep driving."

There was the murmur of confusion and fear from

the back. Colleen could hear pocketbooks being snapped open, coins and jewelry falling into the hat as it was passed forward.

Sly moved slowly into the aisle. Colleen watched the gigolo take hold of the collar of Sly's suitcoat, putting the gun to his head as they danced by each other in the narrow aisle. "You want your brains all over the floor, just fuck with me."

One of the old ladies gasped.

The gunman now stood beside Everett. Sly knelt and raised the seat cushion from the settee, exposing the safe.

Everett was moaning, downshifting, as they began to climb toward the center of the bridge. Colleen saw it all, Sly, the gigolo, and out the window, beyond the concrete abutments that edged the bridge, nothing but water. They slowed as they climbed.

"I got to get my keys," Sly said, on his knees.

"Just do it slowly."

Sly reached into his pocket and came out with a key ring. She watched as he put his hand inside the settee.

"Wait!"

Sly looked up. The gunman walked toward him. "Let me look inside there first." Everett changed gears again, grinding down.

The gigolo was leaning over the settee when Everett hit the brakes. There were screams; people fell out of their seats into the aisle as Everett twisted the steering wheel to the right and at twenty-five miles an hour plowed the bus into one of the abutments at the top of the bridge.

The gigolo fell forward, his gun going off when he hit the floor, the bullet shattering the windshield.

Colleen hit the dividing panel between the front of her seat and the steps leading down to the door. Bruised but uninjured, she was able to pull herself up just as Sly came off the floor with the gun that she had seen mounted inside the settee. She watched as Sly jabbed the point of one wing-tipped shoe into the gigolo's groin, then put the barrel of the gun against the side of his head.

"How 'bout I widen your earhole for you," Sly said.

*A*T LEAST IT HAD STOPPED SNOWING. THE TEMPERATURE climbed a little bit, John Brown thought, and he could almost picture himself sitting by the pool of the Omni Hotel in downtown Miami, sipping cold drinks and trying to score with the rich babes around the pool while their husbands sat inside in air-conditioned conference rooms. Almost. If he kept his eyes closed, but he couldn't keep his eyes closed forever.

Fat Boy was running a regular coolie service, bearing women up here. Funny what a gun going off in your ear could get a guy charged up to do. Carl would go off around noon, tromping through the snow in his new galoshes, pick one up, bring her back in a cab, then send her on her way when Brown had finished with her. Later in the evening, and again at night, Carl repeated the process without ever complaining. However, it was only the second day of this arrangement.

Thinking it might make Fat Boy happier, Brown had even offered to let him share. "You want seconds?" Brown asked, bringing one of the girls out of his room.

Carl's face had begun to glow like someone had just held a heat lamp up to it, and he turned and walked away. Brown laughed.

They were not bad-looking girls, and they were young. Nothing like Jeannie, but it was better than sitting up here beating off and going crazy. Maybe the next time when Carl got back from getting this first one of the morning out, Brown would have him pick up two and bring them both back together. Jesus. He'd never been able to get Jeannie to go for that.

Brown was sitting at the kitchen table cleaning the .45 when Carl came back in.

"What's it like out there?" Brown asked.

"An ice rink," Carl said. "You need skates or snowshoes to get around on. It's below zero right now and going down. I don't want to go back out today."

"I was thinking just once more, maybe having you pick up two for me."

"What are you, a sex maniac?" Carl had taken off his coat and come into the kitchen. He went to the cupboard and got an unopened box of cookies. Brown knew the whole box would be gone when Fat Boy finished.

"Look at it this way," Brown said. "You don't have to worry about me shooting the place up, maybe getting hurt."

"We both got something to worry about."

Brown smiled, watching Carl pump cookies into his mouth and light the stove under the coffee. He wondered if Carl had ever had any fun, just enjoyed life for a while.

"What have we got to worry about now?"

"Company."

Brown was reassembling the revolver. He stopped, turned and looked at Carl. "What are you talking about?"

"A guy's been sitting in his car down there yesterday and today. I go out, he pretends like he's backing in or just pulling out. Today he's in a different spot, but it's the same car and the same guy. You think he's just sitting out there enjoying the weather?"

Looking at the .45, Brown thought about Frank Bishop's call. He had warned Carl that somebody might be back on his trail. But how? He'd moved in here the day after he'd shot the guy who had showed up outside his door at the other place. A fucking bounty hunter; he'd gone through the guy's pockets and found his ID.

Since Carl had been here, Brown hadn't been out of the house. So maybe Fat Boy led the sonofabitch here. One thing he knew for certain: he didn't feel like taking any more chances with somebody else trying to take him. The odds against him were getting slimmer all the time.

"Make one more trip for me," Brown said, looking up at Carl. "Check the guy out. See if you can't force him to show his hand."

Craig was cold and cramped. And bloated after nothing more to eat than snack food and coffee. The guy in the camel-hair coat had come and gone three times. Each time he came back to the house he had a different woman with him. Even though there was something familiar about all of them, something in the way they dressed and moved. Their looks; the use of makeup. He was ready to bet a week of sitting in this car that they were hookers. He was even willing to put up another week in the car that they weren't going into the house to do it with Camel-Hair. He was only the escort, the procurer, the pimp: Colleen Bishop's brother, Carl, bringing home a little treat. Craig thought of the tape he had of Brown having sex on the phone—the guy was wild, and Carl was just keeping him satisfied.

Now, if he could only figure out some way of getting into the house without being seen. He thought about calling the detective at MUC headquarters. Flushing Brown out. But then Brown would be theirs, and Craig would go home empty-handed.

No, the way in the house was through Carl Bishop, Craig convinced now that was who the fat guy in the camel-hair coat was, and also convinced that he was the weak link. But time was running out. If he hadn't been spotted yet, he soon would be. Nearly twenty-four hours he'd been sitting here. He couldn't risk waiting around, just hoping Brown would come out. If he was in there and going to come out, Brown wouldn't have Carl bringing women back to the house, Craig reasoned.

And it did sound reasonable. But if he intercepted Carl on his next pickup trip, he still had to solve the problem of getting into the house.

There was something else. He had promised Colleen that he wasn't interested in Carl, that he wasn't after him, and there was no reason for Carl to be hurt. Why was he worrying about that? He'd made hundreds of promises he couldn't keep; it was how this business worked. There was something about the girl,

Colleen, that stayed with him: he wanted to be able to keep that promise. But in the final analysis, whether Carl got hurt or not was going to depend on Carl.

He was coming out of the house right now. In the rearview mirror Craig watched him turn out of the gate and begin walking cautiously up the street, toward the car.

Colleen checked into the Carlyle Hotel on Miami Beach with its curves and scallops and its staff wearing starched white shirts, bow ties, their dark hair slicked back, looking like they'd stepped out of a 1920s movie. Balmy tropical breezes and the pastel shades of the Art Deco renaissance. What more could you ask for in the middle of February? For starters, how about some stability? In the absence of that, a drink would help, she thought.

She had called Julius the night before from the Keys to tell him she was coming today. She had spent the night, with the old people on the bus, in Marathon. Thankfully, none of them had had a heart attack. The only person seriously hurt was Everett, who had been hospitalized with internal injuries and a concussion. She felt sorry for him; he hadn't wanted to be on the bridges in the first place. In a sense, he had saved them. Sly would have to pay for everybody to get home and hope that no one sued him, although he said he had insurance. The bus was towed back to Marathon.

There was a message from Julius at the hotel desk when she checked in. He would be at the Strand from six until around eight, and after that she could find him back on the porch of his residence, front row, sixth chair from the right, next to an old lady and a checkerboard. Colleen smiled and looked at her watch: six-twenty. She followed the bellhop, who showed her up to her room and gave her directions for getting to the Strand, which was only a few minutes walk from the Carlyle.

By seven she had showered and changed clothes and was on the street breathing the warm, moist Miami air as she walked to the restaurant to meet Julius.

He sat at the bar in the large, open room. She had known him all her life and he never seemed to change. He looked elegant, she thought, so tall and thin, sitting there in a bright flowered shirt, leaning into the bar. His hair still had some color, and if she didn't know him, she would never have guessed that he was seventy-one. Their eyes met in the mirror behind the bar and he stood up.

"I thought you weren't going to make it. I've had two of these," he said, kissing her and motioning to his drink. "Bombay gin, no vermouth, three olives. They make me feel like fifty again. I usually don't have three. When I start feeling like I'm thirty there's going to be trouble. I don't mind dying, I just don't want to hurt myself in the process."

"Don't be silly," Colleen said. "You aren't going to die, you haven't even grown up yet." She ordered scotch from the bartender.

"That never stopped anybody from dying." One corner of his mouth turned up in a familiar half grin. "You know, not too many decades ago if you lived to be fifty you were beating the odds. A man had maybe twenty, thirty years at most to make his mark in life and then it was over. Now they keep you hanging around forever. You're successful, then you spend a lifetime just trying to keep from getting bored. You're a failure, then you have to shoot yourself to get out of the misery. I say to hell with medical science."

"Julius, I don't want to hear that." He had no way of knowing that she'd been in the hospital getting her

73

stomach pumped at Christmas. And she wasn't going to tell him.

"I know. I'm a terrible cynic. I'm also talking too much. Tell me what happened to you."

She told him about Sly and the trip down.

"Sly Gallanti," Julius said. "I thought he was still inside."

"You know him?"

"He's a legend. Worked for the Gambino family before he went to jail, and it's hard to believe that when Sly was just a kid he started out with Capone."

"I can believe anything now," she said. "But when I first met him he seemed so . . ."

"Nice? In the old days they called him the gallant Gallanti."

"I liked him. . . . I gave him your address. He may look you up when he gets the bus fixed and comes back through. He wasn't sure he remembered you."

"It's crazy, isn't it, the two of us, Sly and me, this age, trying to start over with new schemes."

"All right, Julius, tell me about it. What have you got up your sleeve?"

"I'll tell you over dinner. Let's take a table. You can order another drink and I'll see if they've got any food soft enough for me to chew."

She followed him into the dining room, where they were seated at a table for two. A waiter brought them menus and Colleen asked for another scotch. Julius studied the menu. When she was growing up she must have spent more time with him than with Frank. On the weekends he'd take her to the zoo, Coney Island, always buying her stuff; spoiling her, Frank said. Then, when he moved to Miami, it all stopped. Julius would talk to her on the phone, but it wasn't the same. There were other things in her life, like boys, and they lost contact for a while, although Julius always sent things, usually things that she'd outgrown; it wasn't until the last three years, when she was living on her own, that they reestablished close contact again.

"I'd love to be able to sink my teeth into a pork chop," Julius said, still looking at the menu. Although Jewish, Julius was a confirmed atheist. He looked up at her. "So what's Frank up to?" he asked.

"You know Frank doesn't talk to me," she said, "but I think he's in trouble."

"Nothing new."

Colleen sipped her scotch. It wasn't until a few years or so ago that she'd known that Julius worked for Meyer Lansky. She'd always just thought of him as an accountant, an ordinary bookkeeper, as Frank said; a magician with numbers. By the time she found out differently, Lansky was dead and Julius retired. Like Frank, he hadn't talked about business. Now she wasn't sure how much she really wanted to know.

"This is different," Colleen said. "He seems worried. Which isn't like Frank."

"The best thing you can do is stay out of it," Julius said.

"I think I'm already in it." She told him about Craig Chappell.

When she finished, Julius looked at her like she had just confessed to murder. He said, "And you sent the guy to Canada? Why'd you do that?"

"I believed him," Colleen said. "It seemed like the right thing to do."

"What about Carl?"

"Chappell isn't interested in Carl."

Julius shook his head. He was taking this seriously. "People get hurt just for being in the wrong place at the wrong time. Who's the guy Carl's protecting?"

"I think his name is John Brown."

"Jesus, Johnny Brown? What the hell does he need Carl for? Brown can take care of himself."

"Is it that bad?"

"If something happens to Carl it will be. Nobody would give a damn if John Brown took a fall, but you know how Frank feels about Carl. What did you tell Frank?"

"Nothing," Colleen said. "He tried to dig stuff out of me but I didn't tell him anything."

"Good," Julius said. "I think it would be better to stay clear of Frank for a while. I'll talk to him if necessary."

"Is there a chance he could go to jail?"

"Frank? Are you kidding?" Julius reached across the table and held her hands again. "Frank's his own man, nobody will ever touch Frank Bishop. Besides" —Julius pressed her hands in his—"he knows every judge on the east coast."

The waiter came and took their order. When he'd gone, Julius said: "Let's talk about my next business deal before I retire permanently."

"The book on Lansky?"

"That's just to get the capital together," Julius said. "Lansky's got to be a best-seller. The inside story from an insider. We write some sample chapters and ask for a fifty-thousand-dollar advance. How does that sound?"

"Optimistic, but I'm listening."

"Good. With the money, I hit the roulette tables, maybe the Bahamas, maybe Vegas, it doesn't matter."

"You really haven't grown up, have you?"

"Listen now. With fifty grand and the system I've got, I can make a thousand a day at the tables and only work four or five hours. A couple of months and we've doubled our money."

"And if you lose?"

Julius grinned. "I can't lose. It's a sure thing. What do you think?"

"A risk, but the book idea sounds the least risky."

"Life's a risk. So we start with the book. I'll feed it to you, you put it down on paper. If you can hang around for a month, we'll get enough material together for the first few chapters. The gambling you leave to me."

"Come by the hotel tomorrow," she said. "We'll go to the beach and talk about Lansky."

Their food came. Julius looked down at the plate of mashed potatoes, summer squash, and meat loaf. "Maybe with some of the money I'll let medical science get me a set of teeth so I can eat something besides baby food," he said.

_____ *Eight*

CRAIG OPENED THE CAR DOOR AGAINST A FROZEN mound of snow and stepped into the cold. His face and hands were stung by the sub-zero temperature and his knees ached. Carl Bishop, twenty-five yards away, swayed under the dim street lighting as he slowly made his way up the icy sidewalk, clutching the snow-encrusted iron fence railings for support.

Craig climbed over the snowbank to the sidewalk, his hands in the pockets of his coat. As Bishop approached, Craig edged enough of his right hand from his pocket so that Carl would be able to see Barry's Smith & Wesson.

Ten feet separated them. The rest of the street was empty.

"I've been watching you," Craig said when Bishop reached him. "You've either got a hungry snake you're feeding or you're trying to reform the women you've been bringing up there. I'm betting on the hungry snake."

Bishop stopped even with him, still holding the fence spike. "Who the hell are you?"

"A friend of Colleen's, Carl."

Craig watched Carl's face. It was a baby face, soft, fat, and except for the eyes, without expression. The eyes showed surprise and then fear, like a kid suddenly trapped in something he shouldn't have been doing, fearful of the consequences. He thought about what Colleen said: dust him with snow, he would make a great snowman, the eyes like pieces of coal.

And like a kid, Craig was certain that Carl would try to bluff his way out of it. And did. "I don't know what you're talking about," he said.

Craig was ready for him. "I'm talking about John Brown sitting in that house down the street while you pimp for him," he said.

"I don't know any John Brown." Carl turned and started to walk back the way he'd come.

"Hold it," Craig said. He stepped in front of him. "Look down at my right hand before you make any dumb decisions."

Carl looked. "What do you want with me?"

"I want to go with you. Pick up the girl and take her back to the snake."

"Fuck you," Carl said.

"Take a couple seconds and think about it. Help me

79

keep my promise to Colleen. I told her I wouldn't hurt you. But one way or the other I'm taking Brown."

Carl would weigh in close to three hundred, Craig thought. It was a lot of weight to throw around, but Carl had a hard time sounding tough. "You got the wrong guy," he said. But there was no conviction in his voice. Craig fell in with him and they began walking up the street together.

"Where do you get the girls?"

"There's a strip joint up on Park."

At the corner of Villeneuve there was a snowbank and nothing for Bishop to hold onto as they crossed the street. The street was clear, but snow and ice still covered the sidewalks. As they got to the opposite corner, Craig put his hand on Bishop's arm. Bishop walked like an old man, a fat old man, his feet spread wide, as he tried to avoid the icy patches.

They walked three or four blocks that way, Carl hanging onto the iron fences fronting the small snow-covered yards along the sidewalk, hanging on to Craig like a little kid when they crossed streets. They turned left on St. Viateur and walked a block up to Park Avenue. There was a strip joint there with a big flashing neon sign in the shape of an arrow pointing into the place and the silhouette of a naked girl. The sign also advertised nude dancers in English and French.

Carl went in ahead of him. It was like every other strip joint he'd ever been in. There was a bar and a stage with chairs around it, where customers could take their drinks and get a close-up of the perfor-mance. Craig let his eyes get used to the dark interior. There was a girl on the stage, lights flashing on her white skin. She squatted on her heels, naked, at the edge of the stage, the narrow ribbon of dark hair between her legs no more than ten inches from the face of the man who sat gawking up at her.

People greeted Carl as he came in, the big spender, the regular customer. Christ, two and three times a day he was in here taking women out like it was a fast-food carryout joint.

They went to the bar and sat down. Carl ordered a Coke. Craig asked for a shot of dark rum. Moments later two half-clothed women—girls really, Craig thought—joined them. They didn't look more than nineteen, twenty. The dark-haired one with the button nose and a French accent asked Craig if he would buy her a drink. Flipping her hair back from her face, pouty but cute.

"We're just passing through," Craig said. "My friend here's looking for someone to go home with him."

Carl had his back to Craig, talking to the other girl, whose hair was red, or maybe blond. It was hard to tell in this light.

"I go 'ome with your friend. Is not for him, is for another man."

"A snake," Craig said.

"Pardon?"

"Nothing." He reached in his pocket and took out the picture of John Brown that he'd gotten from Les Granger in Miami. He showed it to the girl. "Is that the guy?"

"Yes," she said, looking, no hesitation.

"You like him?"

"No. Is kinky."

Craig put his hand on Carl's shoulder. "You got her? Pay for the drinks and let's get out of here."

"She's got to put some clothes on," Carl said.

The blonde or whatever she was walked away.

"I go 'ome with you," the other girl said to Craig.

"Not this trip, sweetheart," Craig said.

She shrugged but smiled. "I like your accent," she said. "It is cute."

They walked back the way they had come, the girl between them, Carl supporting himself by holding onto the fences. While they had waited for the girl to come back with her street clothes on, Craig explained to Carl how it was going to work. When they approached the house, Craig would be walking a few paces behind them, so if Brown were looking out the window, he'd see Carl and the girl together, nothing out of the ordinary. Craig would hang back, watching the window, and wait until Carl had gone in the gate and up on the steps of the porch before coming in. Just don't try anything, he told Carl, saying, "I can move faster than you, a lot faster."

The first time John Brown was picked up by the police was in Jersey City. He'd been working a picket line there; a bunch of goddamn old broads packing flower bulbs had gone on strike. The Dutchman they worked for had hired scab labor to take their place. Brown was the only man on the picket line; the union he worked for sent him in to keep the girls fired up.

He kept them fired up, all right.

One scab crossed the picket line and he told her that her snatch smelled like rotten fish and her mother was a whore. He couldn't believe it, she came after him swinging her purse above her head like it was a goddamn hatchet. Fending off the purse, he accidentally grabbed her wrist. The next thing, she's down on the ground screaming for the cops. And wouldn't you know it, the cops are right around the corner.

The scab complained, the cops took Brown to the

station, held him for two, three hours. They kept asking him what his name was, and he kept telling them, John Brown. So they held him in a room, ran a computer check on him, and every so often they would say, "What's a nice wop with a WASP name like you doing in Jersey City?"

Shit. They wouldn't have believed him if he'd told them he was born in a swamp in Florida. He told them again he worked for the union and if they didn't want to believe it they could call his mother. Where, they wanted to know, Sicily?

No sense of humor. Still, he had the last laugh. They were about to let him go after two hours, and he said, listen, what kind of cops are you guys, anyway? They just stood there staring at him, chewing gum. Brown said, you bring a guy in, question him, run computer checks and don't even search him.

Then he opened his coat and showed them the little snubnose .38 tucked in his waistband. Before they could tackle him, he had his permit out, his name, John Brown, right there. They nearly shit. Said they didn't want to see him again around Jersey City.

Who needs it? Brown asked.

That was the first time. He'd been picked up other times, but never actually charged with anything. Then he'd got in with Frank Bishop and Frank taught him a few things. Like, you can't beat the cops all the time, so join them.

Which is what he did. Just some odd jobs, some information here and there that didn't mean shit to Brown but somehow kept him off the cops' shitlist and later on got him some work with the feds.

Now here he was sitting up in a cold foreign country like a goddamn scared kid on the run. Fuck it. He wasn't going to live like this. He didn't have to live like this.

After Fat Boy went out, Brown packed his clothes into a bag and went to stand at the front window, waiting to see what Carl was going to bring him. What the hell was taking them so long? If the son of a bitch who Carl thought was keeping watch on them was crazy enough to try to take him, Brown would deal with him the way he'd dealt with the last one. Then go out the back over to Park and get a cab to the airport. He stood just back from the window with a good view of the sidewalk, the .45 in his hand, the silencer attached to the long barrel.

They crossed Villeneuve, and halfway down the block Craig let Carl and the girl go ahead of him ten paces. Carl was like something out of an old Laurel and Hardy clip, or one of those comic duos, the fat man skating on thin ice.

They were only four or five houses away from where Brown was now. Craig quickened his step, glancing at the houses, trying to check the windows at 4588. Carl and the girl were at the gate, Carl pushing it open, the snow mounded on either side of the narrow pathway that had been cleared but was now iced over. Carl holding onto the girl's arm, moving slowly step by step.

Craig saw Brown at the window. He had just glanced up to the second-floor windows, almost ready to turn into the gate, not expecting to see anyone, and their eyes locked on one another. It was like he knew, Brown knew, and the two of them could stand there looking at each other, knowing, yet not knowing, wondering who was going to draw first. It was like that. Show time. Showdown time. It was only seconds, but it seemed like minutes. Craig was about to drop his head, keep walking and double back, when he saw the gun in Brown's hand, the gun being raised to point out the window. Then everything got speeded up. What seemed like minutes passing when they looked at each other now happened in a flash.

Craig shouted at Carl and burst through the gate at the same time. Carl turned toward him, losing his balance, the girl screaming as Carl slipped; Craig coming up face to face with him as the gun went off, making a little popping sound and the glass in the window shattered.

Carl took the bullet in the back of the head and fell, dead weight now, into the snow, crushing Craig beneath him. He tried to roll away but Carl fell faster than he'd ever moved in his life. Craig pushed at the dead body, the camel-hair coat against his mouth, snow being forced up his nose as he fought to breathe. Finally he managed to get enough of Carl's weight lifted so he could squeeze himself out, reaching for the gun in his pocket at the same time. He looked at the window. Brown was gone. The girl was running back up the street.

Blood stained the snow around Carl's head. And it was bloody snow that Craig cleaned from his nostrils. The neighborhood was strangely silent, no sounds other than a car passing occasionally. He could no longer even hear the girl.

Craig dug into Carl's overcoat pockets and came out with his keys. He went up onto the porch and peered through the glass panel in the door at 4588. A narrow stairway went up half a dozen steps before twisting to the right and out of his vision. He tried the door. Locked. He opened it with a key and went in, slowly climbing the steps, keeping his back to the wall, Barry's .38 raised. At the top of the steps was another door, this one solid. Craig listened, flattened against the wall. There was no sound inside. He used Carl's other key to open that door.

Lights were on inside. Looking into the hallway and a living room, he listened, waited. Then stepped inside, his back to a wall as he surveyed the house. He could see into the dining room, the kitchen, and at the end of the kitchen, a bedroom. Across from him was another door that opened onto the front bedroom. Empty. The whole house had the feeling of emptiness. Slowly, he made his way through the rooms, checking closets, behind doors, under the beds.

John Brown was gone.

_____ *Nine*

*J*ULIUS SAT ON THE PORCH OF THE C-BREEZE DABBING AT
his runny eyes with a handkerchief; his thin hands
trembled slightly as he lit a cigarette, his narrow,
snap-brimmed straw hat pushed back on his head.
Thinking, you get to seventy-one, you don't measure
your life in years anymore but in seconds, the time it
takes to smoke a cigarette, knowing that with each one
you put out without dropping dead, you are beating
the odds. Fuck it. What a way to live.

"Julius, are you all right?" Colleen asked.

"Just a little tired," he said. Hating it, but thinking

what he really wanted was to go up to his room and take a nap. Jesus Christ, it was barely noon.

The past few days they had spent mornings on the beach sitting under one of those canvas canopies talking about Meyer Lansky. Meyer. If there was ever a guy who led a charmed life, Julius thought, it was Meyer. Colleen had listened, taking notes, while Julius reeled off names, dates, places, and anecdotes for three hours. Colleen questioned him, forcing him to recall exact details, even conversations that Meyer'd had. Which was fine; she was taking the project seriously, but it exhausted him. Maybe a month wasn't enough time; they were just scratching the surface. Four hours a day was the extent of his concentration. He felt like a cripple. Crippled by age.

Julius shifted his gaze from the ocean to the street. Why was it that staring at water always made him think of death?

"Why didn't you ever remarry?" Colleen asked, suddenly shaking his memory awake once more.

He was looking up Ocean Drive, watching people walking in the noon sun, thinking he'd lived through several fashion changes which he'd never paid much attention to; now it appeared people were dressing the way they had three or four decades ago, inspired probably by this Art Deco stuff. "There was only one woman in my life who meant anything," he said. "When she died in '65, I knew I wasn't going to replace her."

"The year I was born."

"What?"

"She died the year I was born," Colleen said.

"Yeah, that's right." He wanted to avoid this. Colleen had a way of picking stuff up. Julius had his eyes on a guy coming down the street in the direction of the C-Breeze.

"Did you go out with women after that?"

"I still go out with women." He laughed. "But they're all after my money."

As the guy walking along the street got closer, Julius had the feeling he was watching an old gangster picture. Something with George Raft. The guy wore a double-breasted suit. In this heat? And carried an elegant walking stick that he tipped forward on alternate steps. Maybe he was an actor, Julius thought. They filmed up and down here all the time.

The guy in the suit slowed as he approached the hotel, glancing at the people on the porch. He was older than Julius had at first thought, pale, like he hadn't been in Florida long. Like he'd come down from Alaska. Julius would bet he was no actor either. He was walking beside the waist-high wall now, looking right at Julius. He stopped in front of them and said, "Julius Stearns?"

Colleen turned and saw him and said, "Sly." She seemed surprised, happy to see him.

Julius stared at him. The suit was worsted, well-worn, a fine pinstripe running through it. If Colleen hadn't been there, he wondered whether he would have recognized Gallanti. Probably not.

"Julius, you old dog. You don't remember your old friends, do you?"

The voice was familiar. Julius stood and offered his hand. Sly leaned forward over the wall, putting his hands on Julius's shoulders and pulling him forward. Sly kissed him on each cheek. The fucking Italians never changed, Julius thought.

"I should have recognized your clothes," Julius said. "Weren't you wearing the same ones thirty years ago?" Sly laughed. "Come up and sit down."

"When did you get here?" Colleen asked when Sly joined them on the porch.

"Today. I drove the bus in from the Keys. All the damage is external, and I can get it fixed faster here."

"How's Everett?"

"He's going to be laid up a while. I had him transferred up here to Jackson Memorial. He couldn't stand Marathon. Being that close to all those bridges and water. He said he's going to retire now. Did she tell you, Julius?"

"Tell me what?"

"That Everett drove for Greyhound for twenty-five years, the last couple of years between Miami and Key West before they built new bridges. Scared to death every time he went down there that he was going to crash and go over the side, plunge into all that water. I knew him in prison when he was serving three years for coming out of his first retirement and getting into armed robbery. He made a better driver than a burglar. We set this thing up in prison, and when I got out I hired him to drive. The first trip to the Keys, his worst nightmare damn near comes true. He plows into the side of the bridge to stop a robbery. A robbery!"

"I heard that part," Julius said. "You're lucky to be alive."

"Did you call Frank?" Colleen asked. "Are you still in business?"

"I called him. We've got a temporary setback, but Frank's still in. I'll drive the bus up when it's fixed, find another driver in New York and we'll try it again."

"What about the trip back up?" Colleen smiled, Sly winked; Julius catching something between them. "All that high-yield investment return you'll be losing out on?"

What was that all about? Julius wondered.

Sly didn't answer. He just stared at Colleen. He

didn't seem angry, more like he was pulled up short. Colleen could do that to people.

"Well, I'll be getting back to my hotel now," Colleen said. "You two probably want to reminisce about the old days. I'll talk to you later," she said to Julius.

"What was that all about?" Julius asked when she was gone.

"She's a smart kid," Sly said. "I like her. She seems to have a hard time with Frank, though."

"Everybody has a hard time with Frank these days. What kind of a deal did he give you?"

"He didn't give me anything. I offered to let him come in on a sure thing. If he didn't pick it up, somebody else would have."

"Bringing tourists to Florida?"

"It's better than that," Sly said.

"The business Colleen was hinting at."

"She was guessing."

"And you aren't talking."

"You know this business as well as I do," Sly said. "The longer you keep your mouth shut, the longer you're gonna live."

"Yeah," Julius said, "between us we've got over a hundred and forty years of silence. When are we going to start talking?"

Sly laughed. "Let's talk," he said. "It's been twenty years, maybe more since I saw you."

"You been inside all that time?"

"Every day of it, but here I am."

"Now you're bragging."

"Listen," Sly said. "I still get a hard-on."

"Good for you. I'll fix you up with one of the gals here. I got one seventy-nine who likes to play checkers. I don't know if she'll go down on you, though."

Sly shook his head. *"Grazie,"* he said. "After twenty years in prison you get other interests."

Julius looked at him, uncertain. "Are you saying what I think you're saying?"

"Probably."

"Sly? The ladies man? You got to be kidding."

"I'm not kidding. It's a matter of economics I guess. Supply and demand. Availability. You understand that. We've got to live in the real world—or the best we can in prison."

Julius couldn't believe it. Finally he laughed. "Well, I guess you got to find it where you can. You won't have any trouble here. South Florida is full of queers."

"Nobody says that anymore," Sly said. "The term is gay."

"I'm too old to learn a new language," Julius said.

"Carl's dead." They were the first words out of Frank's mouth. She had come back to the Carlyle and found his message, and after going up to her room she called him. The first thing she thought of when he said it, Carl's dead, was a heart attack. Overweight. He had eaten himself to death. A purely nervous habit.

Then Frank said, "He was shot in Montreal." And she thought of something else. She heard Craig Simmons Chappell, whatever his name was, as he walked beside her on a cold, windblown New York street saying he wouldn't hurt Carl. He wasn't interested in Carl.

Colleen said, "What happened?"

Frank said, "I just told you what happened."

She felt terribly depressed. She'd been feeling so good for so long recently, she had almost forgotten the depression. Now this. Even though he was her fat brother and she didn't much like him, the idea of him being killed was . . . well, it was depressing. Less than three months ago she'd tried to kill herself, and now

Carl was dead. It made no sense. All she could think to say to Frank was, "I'm sorry."

"You sound like you're apologizing," Frank said.

"No, I don't mean it that way." Couldn't he ever, just once, at a time like this, let up on her?

"Maybe you do," he said.

"What?" What was he saying?

"The police up there called me. Somebody called them and told them about Carl, laying in the snow, shot in the head. A guy from Miami name of Craig Chappell. Ring any bells with you?"

She didn't say anything.

Frank went on. "Isn't that the guy who came to see you? Had all this money to give you from your family. You said he'd made a mistake. Maybe Carl was the one he really wanted to talk to, and you told him where he was."

"No," she said. Just that. She needed to think. Try to remember everything, put this together. She could see where it was leading.

"No, what?"

She ignored his question. "Who killed Carl?" Frank was driving at something, and she wasn't going to let him do it. There was Frank's opinion, and that was law. Nothing else counted. It had been that way with Frank all her life.

"What do you think I'm just telling you?"

"Chappell shot him? And then called the police to tell them about it?"

"Carl's dead. Do you think I care about the intricacies? Chappell killed him. Or Chappell got him killed. What difference does it make?"

"I can see that you've already tried the case and are going for a conviction. What about the Montreal police? Are they going along with you? Have they got Chappell?"

"Colleen, are you defending him? Carl was killed. Chappell left Canada before they could talk to him. Is there something you want to tell me about this guy?"

What good would it do? She wanted to hang up, walk out on the beach, see people doing normal things, get away from death for a while. What was it like growing up in a normal family? she wondered. Everybody wasn't like this. Were they? She said no, she didn't have anything to tell him about Chappell.

Frank hesitated. "All right," he said. "What's done is done. And I will do what I have to do."

"What are you talking about?"

"It doesn't matter," he said. Pause. "This has been a difficult week. A few days ago I get a call from Sly telling me what happened with the bus. Then Carl. Maybe I'm getting old. My judgment's going."

"I'm all right," she said.

"What?"

"In case you were worried about me. I wasn't hurt."

"Carl's dead," Frank said again.

"I'm sorry," she repeated. And she was.

Colleen stripped off her clothes and stepped into the shower. The water felt good, cleansing, soothing. She cried, let the tears flow as the water gushed over her. And that too was cleansing. Carl was her brother; Carl was dead. And she had led someone straight to him. She leaned against the tile and sobbed.

When she stopped crying she knew what she had to do; she wanted to know what happened in Montreal and she intended to find out. She would begin by asking Craig Chappell. She couldn't allow Frank to hold her responsible for this. Not if she were going to be able to get on with her own life.

Ten

*I*T WAS EVENING WHEN BROWN WALKED INTO FRANK Bishop's building on West Twelfth. Frank was going to shit when he saw him, but Brown had already figured out how he was going to handle the Irishman.

In the foyer a blue-haired receptionist sat behind inch-thick Plexiglas while an electronic video camera monitored the outer office. Brown smiled, waved, walked over to the glass and said, "Mabel, how you doin'? Long time no see. The old man still in?"

"He's on the phone," Mabel said.

Brown sat down in one of the chairs against the wall

and picked up a back issue of *People* from a small table beside him. He thumbed through it, read something about the marital problems of Prince Charles and Lady Di, thinking, Christ, all Frank had to do was put in a fish tank, take out the Plexiglas and the camera, and you'd think you were at the dentist.

Frank Bishop might remove a guy's teeth, or have somebody else remove them was more like it, Brown thought, but he sure as hell wasn't going to fix any.

Brown wondered why nobody had ever asked him to drive a car for Prince Charles. He could take the bonny Prince around Florida, show him some sights he'd never see in Palm Beach where he sometimes came to play polo. He could show Di some sights too. Take her back into the swamps and let her play with some 'gators. Let her play with *his* 'gator.

It came to him why nobody had ever asked him to drive a car for Prince Charles when Mabel said, "Mr. Brown, you can go in now." He walked across the carpeted floor to an inside door. Mabel pressed a buzzer that released the lock and Brown opened the door onto a corridor that led to Frank's inner sanctum.

Frank was standing there beside his secretary's desk, waiting for him when Brown walked up. He didn't look surprised to see him at all. Maybe angry. He just stood there, his hands clasped together like he was praying.

"You got a lot of balls," Frank said.

Brown had been waiting to see Frank's face, get some measure of his mood before deciding how he should play this. Maybe Frank wouldn't have heard yet about Carl. Then Brown could break it to him gently. Tell him what had happened. He could see right away that wasn't the case. Frank knew. "You heard about Carl, I guess," he said.

"I'm sitting here in the office and some cop in Montreal calls up out of the blue to tell me he's dead. If that's what you call hearing about him."

"Yeah," Brown said. "I thought I might get here before that happened. Be the one to break it to you."

"You're all heart, Johnny. Now just tell me what the hell happened up there."

"Carl spotted some guy practically living in his car on the street. An Eskimo wouldn't have been caught out in that cold unless he had a good reason—like surveillance. He was just like the one before who showed up there. Carl went out to talk to him. I don't know what happened. I'm standing in the window waiting for Carl to come back when the guy comes in the front gate, Carl ahead of him. They both looked up, must have seen me in the window. The guy dropped down on the snow, pulled a gun and shot Carl in the back of the head. It was over in a second."

"That's the way it happened, Johnny . . . you sure you got your story straight?"

"Frank, what're you talking about?"

"The cop in Montreal had a different story."

"Yeah? He's standing there on the street watching it. Man, the street was empty."

"I guess he must have heard somebody else's version. His version was you killed Carl."

Brown laughed. "What am I gonna kill Carl for?"

"I don't know. Maybe you didn't mean to."

"Frank, when did I ever shoot somebody I didn't mean to? Look, you want me to, I'll walk the fuck outta here. After all these years you don't believe me . . ."

"Why'd you come back here?"

"I'm going to sit up there and wait on the cops to start asking me questions? Or some bozo to come in and drag me back here in handcuffs? Fuck that place. I can get lost right here in this city."

Frank stared at him. He seemed older, grayer than the last time Brown had seen him. Abruptly, Frank turned and walked into the boardroom with its long conference table, where Brown had often met with Frank and Carl when they were planning an operation. He'd seen Frank pissed off plenty of times, yelling at whoever was the object of his anger, sometimes Brown, but he had never seen the old man mad at Carl. Even though in many ways, Brown thought, Frank regarded him more like the son Frank wanted Carl to be; tougher, more independent, and less afraid of life. Although Brown had never talked about that with Frank, he had also never misjudged their relationship: Carl was family, Brown just worked there.

Now maybe things would be different without Carl. The dumb fuck, just an accident waiting to happen.

Brown followed him into the boardroom. Frank stood across the table from Brown, his back turned to him. "You don't have to hide anymore," he said. "They've dropped the charges against you. Both of you could have been standing here right now."

Brown didn't say anything.

"I want you to get him, the guy who killed Carl. His name's Craig Chappell and I want him dead. You got nothing else to think about between now and then."

As Brown went out he remembered something. The reason nobody ever asked him to drive for Prince Charles was they knew John Brown only drove for kings. He liked that.

Craig was back in Miami less than a week, after being hassled by the cops in Montreal who suggested with less than usual politeness that he stay out of

Canada. The first day back Les Granger at the State Attorney's office called.

"How's it going?" Les asked. Like they were old buddies.

"Slow," Craig said. "I should have known about Bishop earlier. It would have saved a lot of work. It's going to take some time now."

"Well, you can forget it," Granger said.

"Forget what?"

"John Brown."

Craig held back, telling himself to take it easy, the past week or two he'd been under stress. Don't go off the deep end. He looked around the office. The tape recorder—he still had the tape with the X-rated conversation between Brown and his girlfriend—was on the table, and above it a photograph of Barry he'd had enlarged and framed, showing him clowning around on the back of the boat. The same boat he'd scattered Barry's ashes from. Forget it? He'd like to, but it might not be that easy.

"What happened?" Craig asked. Cool. No emotion.

"The charges against him have been dropped."

"No kidding. What about his bail bond?"

"Paid," Granger said.

"Is the guy lucky or what?"

Granger laughed. "You might say that."

"You want to talk about it?"

"No," Granger said.

"Did Bishop have a hand in this?"

"Like I told you," Granger said, "forget it. Don't go off the deep end on this one."

"Funny," Craig said. "I was just telling myself the same thing."

He decided to take Granger's advice, and said to hell with it. He drove down to the Keys for a couple of days, thinking he might figure things out, make some decisions about where he was going with the rest of his life. He started drinking in a bar around mile marker 75 near Islamorada in mid-morning, and by the time he hit Key West at noon was glad there was no more road to travel. He'd come to the end of the line. Mile zero.

The sleepy tourist town that he remembered from fifteen years ago when he'd first brought Barry, still a kid then, down here to go fishing, was trying its hardest to become a resort, and Jesus, he couldn't believe what had happened to this place, making a fool of itself in the process. Every hotel room was full, he had no reservations, and so he slept in his car—when he slept.

He scored with a girl in one of the downtown bars he hit. He asked her if she wanted to go back to his place.

"Where's that?" she asked.

"A place on the beach," he said.

The girl smiled, high and happy, and they got in his car. He drove her to the Atlantic Ocean on the other end of town, a small patch of sand between two large beachfront buildings, one of them a large old house that had been turned into a restaurant.

"Where you?" she asked. A thin smile. Eyes turned inward.

He pointed to the sand. She looked, then turned in the seat to him. "On—on the beach?"

"Yeah, with the biggest water bed you've ever been in . . ."

She thought a minute, then laughed and said, "Dig it, let's go," and had her clothes off by the time she hit the water.

Two days later he drove out of town, hung over,

disgusted both with himself and the tourist trap he was forsaking, and still without any plans, any direction.

He thought about women on the way back to Miami. Forty, and he was living alone. He wasn't much good at intimate relationships, he guessed. He liked women, he just couldn't seem to get close to them—didn't want to get close, maybe. They started making motions like they wanted to stay over a few days, or they were cooking meals two or three nights in a row, and he got nervous. Maybe he was scared. He didn't want to repeat what he'd been through with his wife that time. One guy he knew, a girl hung around longer than he wanted her, he'd take the bathroom door off its hinges. They were gone in a flash when they couldn't find privacy in a bathroom.

Craig didn't know what he wanted. He wasn't even sure he wanted to go on with this business anymore. He felt tired, old. The fire had gone; the enthusiasm just wasn't there. What the hell was this, some kind of mid-life crisis? One thing, he had to make a living.

And what about the stuff with John Brown? What was he going to do about that? He had no answers.

He went home, slept in a bed for twelve hours for the first time in two nights, reluctantly dragging himself to the office around noon the next day after a solid breakfast and several cups of strong black coffee.

There were messages on his answering machine, but only one of them, repeated three times during his three-day absence, interested him.

Colleen Bishop was in Miami and had left a number where she could be reached.

When she told him about Frank's call, Julius said he would talk to Frank, try to calm him down. Colleen

John Leslie

was glad she didn't have to face Frank. She felt badly
enough about Carl without having to be around Frank
when he went into one of his tirades. Carl had so
many strikes against him—if he'd somehow gotten
out from under Frank much earlier, she wondered
would he have turned out differently?

Frank hadn't mentioned a funeral. If she went up
there for that, then she would be face to face with him.
She wasn't sure she could do it right now. If she chose
not to go to the funeral, Julius said he would support
her decision. He was so fatalistic. What difference did
it make to the dead who went to their funerals? he
said.

The time she spent with him she enjoyed. He was
kind and understanding. And surprisingly, she loved
listening to his stories about Lansky. They were
wonderful. She was certain they would make a good
book. She was even thinking of looking for an apartment here. She could spend the rest of the winter in
Miami helping Julius and doing the reading she had to
do for her own work. It was warm, she could spend
time in the sun. Keep the healing process going.

Except there was still Craig Chappell. She was on
again, off again about that. If she called him, then she
was keeping the whole thing going; if she didn't call,
then she might never learn the truth.

Several days went by since Frank had called and
told her about Carl. Finally she'd tried to reach Craig.
Maybe he wouldn't even see her, talk to her. He had
no reason to. She kept getting his answering machine;
he never returned her calls. She persisted. If he had
killed Carl, it would be like signing his own death
warrant as far as Frank was concerned.

She came back to her hotel after cutting short a
morning session with Julius. She told him she had

102

some things to do, but the truth was she found herself thinking all the time about Chappell. When she picked up her key at the desk, there was a phone message from Craig Chappell. She went to her room and called him.

"Small world," she said when he answered the phone. "First your brother, then mine. Both in the same city. Total strangers."

"Yeah," he said. "And here we are."

"And here we are," Colleen repeated. "I think we ought to meet again. For old time's sake."

"Neutral territory?"

"You name it," she said. "I'm in the Carlyle Hotel on Ocean Drive."

"How about the beach out front?"

"Safety in numbers, is that it?"

Craig said, "Give me a time."

"When can you get here?"

"I'll be on the beach in twenty minutes."

"Will you recognize me?"

"Sure. You've got brown eyes."

As it turned out, he didn't have to recognize her. She recognized him. He'd been on the beach maybe ten minutes, walking along getting sand in his shoes, when she came up behind him and put a finger in his back.

He turned. "Is that supposed to be funny?" he asked her. There were a lot of people on this stretch of beach, most of them, it appeared, older Beach residents, their skin dappled dark brown like old, polished shoes. Colleen was wearing shorts with sneakers and a striped T-shirt. She wasn't smiling.

"No, not funny. It's supposed to prove something to you."

"Like what?"

"Frank Bishop thinks you killed Carl," Colleen said.

"And you? What do you think?"

"It doesn't matter what I think. Frank knows you were in Montreal and he holds you responsible."

"John Brown killed your brother. The man I went to find. He shot him, probably trying to kill me, and there was nothing I could do about it."

They were walking along the beach. Colleen, her head down, kicked up sand as she walked. She suddenly stopped and stared out to sea.

"But you happened to be right there with him," she said.

"For a couple of days Carl had been picking up women and taking them back to the house for Brown. I intercepted him. It was the only way I could think of to get inside the house."

"But Carl, the clumsy, overgrown baby, messed it up for you by getting in the way of a bullet meant for you," she said.

Craig shrugged. "I'm telling you what happened. It's the truth."

"And I'm telling you the truth too. Carl was all Frank Bishop had. You shouldn't have to read between the lines. You were there. If Frank says you're guilty, you're guilty."

"What about you?" Craig said. "Frank's got you."

"I don't count. I'm not going to give Frank any Bishop babies."

"Jesus Christ, has your family skipped a century? You're not even Italian."

"The Irish can be just as backward."

"So because you hate your family you came all the way to Miami to warn me about Frank Bishop?"

Colleen turned and faced him. "I didn't come down here to find you. I'm helping a family friend write a book."

"What kind of a book?"

"About Meyer Lansky."

"Jesus Christ."

"That's a friend of Frank's too," Colleen said. "He wouldn't like you taking his name in vain."

Frank Bishop. Meyer Lansky. Who else was going to get into this? he wondered. What was he going to have to do, take on the entire mafia, even the dead ones, because of Carl Bishop?

He thought about calling Les Granger. See if he couldn't build a case against Brown again, maybe even Frank Bishop. No, fuck that. Whatever he did from now on would have to be on his own. Unofficial.

For some reason that made him feel better. He had no doubt he could find Brown. Like he'd told Granger, it would just take more time, and he wouldn't be paid for it.

Unless Bishop were willing to pay. There was a thought, an idea worth considering.

Craig decided to consider it from his boat. It was Friday. He'd fucked away most of the week, he might as well really do it in. After stopping at home to pick up his gear in Kendall, he drove to Dinner Key Marina in Coconut Grove. And after fueling up the twenty-four-foot Grady White, he headed out looking for a weedline and dolphin.

By evening he had the Igloo cooler half filled with fish. He came in toward shore to a protected anchorage, filleted and cooked one of the fish with some potatoes, fixed a tomato and onion salad, drank a beer and generally began feeling better about life. Which was probably a mistake, he thought. The Chappell motto had always been expect the worst and you won't ever be let down.

The next morning he caught a few yellowtail, brought the boat to the dock around noon, hosed it down, and gave some fish away before getting into his car to head home.

Eleven

FINDING CHAPPELL WAS EASY. AS EASY AS LOOKING IN
the goddamn phone book. C. Chappell with an address in Kendall. Brown could practically picture the
house, on one of those subdivisions, tracts, lots, next
to the malls. They all looked the same. The guy
probably living there with his wife and a couple of
kids. Brown thought of something that would be fun.
Grab all those suburbanites starting with the Chappell
family and take them down to Flamingo Key where
Brown was born. Let them see what Florida, South
Florida, really was. Except that was different now

too—run by the state park service, not like it was when he'd been growing up there the first thirteen years of his life. Until his mother moved to Miami after leaving his father, a real swamp creature who holed up in Flamingo when he wasn't smuggling drugs into the state.

What wasn't different though was the Everglades. He could take them back in there and lose their ass in a swamp no more'n a hour from their cute little home in Kendall. Instead of a yard filled with kids' toys, he'd pitch them next to a 'gator hole, and then walk away and see how long they survived.

He was getting carried away, Brown thought. In the yellow pages there was Chappell Bros. Security, Inc. with an address in downtown Miami that Brown recognized as being in the bail-bond area of town. He tried phoning the number and got an answering machine. From Jeannie's he called Chappell's house day and night for a couple of days without getting an answer. Then he asked to borrow her car. She didn't need it because he got her to quit her job. "I'm going to take care of you," he told her. "Like you always wanted, right?" She was a hostess in a lounge at the Omni Hotel, where he'd met her a couple years ago; it was a job she could always get back anytime she wanted it. Besides that she had a rich mother up in Delray Beach who was always sending her money. He didn't want to have to work around some shift worker's hours; not after what he'd been through in Montreal. He wanted her there when he wanted her there.

"What do you need the car for?" she asked.

"I'm looking for a guy."

"Anybody I might know?"

"I doubt it."

He thought about telling her, yeah, the guy who had your phone bugged all the time I was in Canada, but that was going to upset her. He had guessed, and as it turned out, correctly, that they'd found him the first time through the wiretap. He could have told her that from Canada after the guy—he now thought of him as Chappell One—showed up. But what good would it have done? After the incident with Chappell One, Brown had stopped calling Jeannie anyway. If she'd had the wiretap removed, it would just have disturbed her and alerted Chappell Two. Who, as it turned out, had tapped into another source to find Brown the second time. He'd like to know who that was.

"How long will you be gone?" Jeannie asked.

She was beginning to get on his nerves. "Until I find him," he growled.

Which was one day of surveillance in Kendall outside the guy's house. And if you stopped to think about that, it was pretty funny, Brown thought. Since not long ago Chappell had been out in front of Brown's house. Look who got the best deal. He would take a day of this to any amount of time sitting in a snowbank in Montreal. What he'd like to do, Brown thought, is be standing in the picture window when Chappell decided to come home. Seeing him there holding the .45, the guy would shit.

Chappell showed up midday Friday and was only in the house half an hour. When he came out he placed a couple of fishing rods in the car and some other gear and drove off. Brown followed him to a convenience store where he made a stop before going on to the marina at Dinner Key.

Brown watched him buy ice and bait that would last a couple of days. Then Chappell took off in the spiffy fishing boat he'd probably bought with bounty money.

But Brown knew now how he was going to deal with Craig Chappell.

* * *

"Julie, I'm worried about Colleen." Frank's voice was solemn, deliberate. Julius had heard him sound like this thousands of times in the past. It meant Frank was looking for sympathy; you were supposed to feel sorry for him, but Frank never just wanted sympathy —it was a means to an end, an emotional trap, and Julius understood Frank well enough to be wary.

"What are you worried about, Frank? She seems fine to me. Carl's death has upset her."

"Colleen's all I've got now. Like in the old days when I first adopted her. I thought she was going to be the only one, the only child we'd ever have."

"I remember," Julius said. "Then Carl came along and Colleen became second fiddle."

"It wasn't like that, Julius. You understand. A son is important in this business. I had hopes Carl would run this place someday."

"Yeah, I understand. And so does Colleen."

"Julie, Julie, Julie. Colleen never wanted for anything. She had everything. I took care of her like she was my own."

"Yeah, but you didn't love her the way you loved Carl. You put her on hold. She knows that. And now Carl's gone, you want her back. I don't know, Frank. She's not a kid anymore."

"She's different. She's got her own way of doing things. She's headstrong."

"Yeah, I wonder where she gets that."

"Julie, what's she doing down there?"

"She's helping me with a book I'm doing on Meyer."

"But is she after you to talk about the past?"

"No," Julius said.

"I'd rather you didn't get into any of that."

"And I rather thought you'd feel that way."

"Dear God, what are you going to do?"

"I don't know," Julius said. It had always pleased Julius in some strange way that he was one of the few men Frank Bishop ever seemed to allow the freedom of choice.

"Well, let me know what you decide," Frank said. "How much loss is a man supposed to take?"

"You're the religious authority," Julius replied. "You should have the answer to that."

"Don't make fun of me, Julie. I'm not in the mood. This business with Carl isn't easy to get over."

"Colleen says you think you know who's responsible."

"I do know. And believe me, the sonofabitch is going to wish he'd never heard of Montreal."

Monday evening Colleen was sitting in the Strand having a drink with Julius. A small TV on the far edge of the counter behind the bar was on. The local evening news at six. Ann Bishop (no relation that she knew) and the entire Eyewitness News Team. The sound was turned down so that it was barely audible above the background noise of the bar. Julius was talking, telling another anecdote about Meyer. In the time she'd been here she must have collected a hundred Meyer Lansky stories. The trouble was, they were disconnected; she was going to have to find a thread that would weave them all together and make something coherent, if they were going to have a book out of this. She was beginning to wonder.

Her thoughts drifted to Julius and Lansky, to Carl ... and Craig Chappell. She was thinking about slipping away, maybe going to a movie by herself or just going back to the hotel to read. She felt like being alone. Suddenly something on the screen caught her attention.

A car was burning on a busy highway. What was so

unusual about it was the speed with which someone was recording the incident. It was as if the cameraman were there before the accident happened.

The car was still moving as the video camera picked it up. It looked as if the car had exploded; its hood was blown off, the driver's door was hanging open—and there was no sign of anyone inside.

Then the camera panned and she saw why it seemed like the accident had just happened. It had. The camera was being held inside a moving van that must have been part of the traffic at the time of the accident. At first she thought it was a movie being filmed on the street. A scene from *Miami Vice,* maybe. But when the burning car came to a halt, the van stopped and the cameraman jumped out, held the camera on the van, picking up the Channel 10 *Eyewitness News* logo. This was real.

The camera swept back along the road, the picture bouncing as the cameraman ran toward a small crowd of people gathered in the middle of the highway. She saw why there was no one in the flaming car as the cameraman reached the crowd; a man was lying in the road. As the camera came in close, Colleen looked into the bloodied face of Craig Chappell. For ten seconds her attention had been riveted to the screen. She said, "My God."

Julius looked around at the screen.

"What's that all about?" he asked.

"I know him. I just talked to him the other day. It's the guy I sent to Montreal to see Carl." The camera pulled back as more people crowded around. The wail of sirens could be heard faintly from the TV.

"You're kidding," Julius said.

"His name's Craig Chappell."

Julius stared at the screen. "Do you know the odds

of something like this happening? You sitting here watching the man who killed your brother get blown out of a car on a Miami highway?"

"He didn't kill Carl," Colleen said.

"Frank says he did."

"Frank's wrong."

"Honey, Frank's never wrong. He may not be God, but he sits at the right hand. If he says this guy, whoever he is—Chappell—killed Carl, then that's the way it is. You can count on it the same way you can count on Frank dealing with it."

"Maybe he just did."

An ambulance, its red lights flashing, was parked on the median. Stretcher bearers were putting Craig Chappell into the back of the ambulance as police directed traffic. It was hard to tell if Chappell was alive or not.

"I can't believe it." Julius sat staring at the screen, shaking his head. "If I lived to be a hundred and ten I wouldn't believe it. Frank's payback, and he gets it live on evening news for everyone to see. Including you."

"Don't give Frank more credit than he deserves." Colleen was shaken. "Maybe it was an accident." But she didn't believe it even as she said it. She finished her drink and stood up.

"Where you going?" Julius asked.

"To find out what happened."

"Colleen, you're better off staying out of this. It's got nothing to do with you."

"I think it's got to do with me. I sent the guy to Montreal."

"Frank's your father," Julius protested.

"No, he isn't. I don't know who my father is and I can't understand why you're protecting Frank, but someday I'll tell you about Frank Bishop and maybe

113

you'll get over defending him." She turned and went out the door.

Jackson Memorial Hospital. Colleen stood at the desk trying to get information about Craig Chappell. He had been in the intensive care unit for twenty-four hours and was in stable condition, a nurse at the desk told her. Visitors, however, were not permitted in an ICU. The nurse studied Craig's file and asked Colleen if she was a family member. No, she said. Did she know any family? Again no. She remembered that both his mother and father and a brother were dead. She didn't know if there was anyone else in the family.

"When can I see him?" Colleen asked.

"Call tomorrow," the nurse said.

She left the hospital, took a cab back to her hotel and immediately called Frank in New York.

When he came on the line she said, "Frank, a few hours ago I saw a car accident on television."

"I always said TV was a bad influence. Worse than being on the streets. You could spend your life on the streets and never see a tenth the awful stuff they show you on the box."

"Frank, you don't understand."

"You're calling me from Miami to talk about some TV show you saw?"

"No, Frank. I'm not talking about a show. I was watching the news with Julius—"

"Dear God, Julius. I'm worried about Julius. You think he might be getting senile, that disease, what is it?"

"Alzheimer's."

"That's it. I don't know I'd pay too much attention to Julius these days."

"Frank, listen to me. A local TV news team here

filmed an accident yesterday. A car blew up and the driver was nearly killed. I saw it on the evening news."

"So?"

"So the guy in the car was Craig Chappell."

"My, my, you don't say. What a coincidence."

"Is it more than that, Frank?"

"Colleen, you sound like you feel sorry for the guy. He was responsible for Carl's death. You want me to get down and kiss his feet?"

"I want you to tell me you didn't have anything to do with that accident."

"You sound distraught. I understand. Carl's gone. It's got us all on edge."

"Tell me, Frank."

Silence.

"Come back to New York and we'll talk," Frank said.

"I won't be back to New York," Colleen said. And hung up.

Brown answered the phone at Jeannie's. It was Frank.

"I hear our friend nearly died in a car accident on TV yesterday."

Brown thought, Jesus, what's the guy got, some satellite dish he can watch every fucking news broadcast in the country? Brown had only watched the thing on Channel 10 last night himself and learned from the hospital this morning that Chappell was still alive.

"Where'd you hear that?" Brown asked.

Frank said, "I got my sources. What happened?"

"You seem to know as much as I do."

"I know the guy's alive," Frank said.

"You ever have a guy hanging over your shoulder when you're trying to do something? You know what it feels like?" Brown asked. "Or maybe you had some other reason for calling." He didn't feel like taking a lot of shit from Frank Bishop now. Or ever, for that matter.

Frank didn't come right back at him the way he usually did, which was just as well. "There is something else," Frank said. "Do me a favor, since you've got time on your hands . . ." He wasn't going to let it go. "Check on a guy for me. We're in a deal together and I got a bad feeling—"

"I've got a bad feeling too," Brown said. "I can't live doing favors."

"Have I ever let you down?" Frank asked. And then got in another shot. "But then I got to turn the question around and ask, have you ever let me down? Don't worry, I'll see you're taken care of."

"Who's the guy?"

"Sylvester Gallanti. Sly for short. He brought a busload of old people and my daughter, Colleen, down to Miami a few weeks ago and ran into some trouble. He's staying in a hotel over on the Beach." Brown wrote down the name of the hotel.

"What do you want me to do?"

"Just assure me," Frank said. "I want to know what he's doing, where he goes, who he sees."

Brown said, "And who you got watching me?"

"You've got a suspicious nature," Frank said. And hung up.

Twelve

*T*ELLING THE CAB DRIVER TO WAIT FOR HIM, HE wouldn't be a minute, Sly, a briefcase dangling from his right hand, went into the paint and body shop where workmen were getting the bus ready to be painted.

Sly looked over the bus, guys working on her with white paper masks that covered the lower half of their faces. Two new headlights had been installed, a windshield replaced, new bumper that had been ordered special and shipped in, and all the dings in the grill hammered out. With paint on her she'd be good as new. A stocky guy in blue work pants and a dirty T-shirt came up to Sly. "Tomorrow, the next day, we should have her ready."

"I think I want the name taken off the sides," Sly said.

They walked around the bus. The guy said, "Sly's Singles?"

"Any problem to paint that out?"

"No problem." The guy grinned. "They all married now, or what?"

"You can't keep 'em apart." He had decided he didn't want any advertising, nothing on there that was going to call attention to the bus. Just another charter deadheading to New York. Risky, but he was going to have to take a chance or lose the connection.

Sly walked to the front of the bus and opened the door. He went on and pulled the door closed behind him. Taking out his keys, he removed the seat cushion on the settee, exposing the safe, and got down on one knee to open it. Then opened the briefcase he'd brought on with him and began filling it with banded packets of hundred dollar bills, five thousand dollars to a packet. When he finished he counted the packets. There were twenty of them laid neatly in the briefcase. Sly took the nine-millimeter handgun off its bracket and put it into the briefcase, then snapped the case closed and replaced the settee cushion.

He walked off the bus, closed the door behind him and walked out to the cab. "Back to the hotel," he said.

Brown would have loved to press his face against one of the smoked windows on the bus while Gallanti was on there. See what went in or maybe came out of that briefcase. Sure that was what happened, because

118

otherwise why would he be carrying the damn thing in here in the first place?

Brown followed in Jeannie's car as the cab worked its way back over to Collins Avenue and Gallanti's hotel. Brown parked, watched as Gallanti paid the driver then went inside. Brown gave him a couple minutes then went in himself. Nothing better to do, he'd hang around here for a while and wait for Gallanti to move again. If the guy left without the briefcase, Brown knew ways to get into his room and satisfy his curiosity; if Gallanti went out with the briefcase, then Brown would follow him, maybe pick up the .45 from the car and stick it in Gallanti's back. And say what? "Your money or your life"— something dumb like that? He'd think about it while he waited, try to come up with something more original.

"You don't look so hot," Colleen said.

There might have been the hint of a smile turning up the corners of Craig Chappell's mouth, she couldn't tell. More likely it was pain that contorted his features. He lay there, his right arm in a cast, stitches tying part of his face together above one eye; more stitches below his lower lip, which was swollen and blue. Head injuries, a broken arm, multiple contusions. Not bad for a guy who'd been catapulted from his car onto a busy highway. He should have been dead.

Colleen told him that. "You're supposed to be dead," she said.

He looked at her and blinked. A nurse came in, read his chart and went through her routine of recording his vital signs. "He's got a long way to go before he'll make good company," she told Colleen. "Are you family?"

"A friend."

"The first one. Nobody's claimed him." The nurse patted Craig's sheeted foot as she walked around the end of the bed. "A real loner, I guess." She left the room.

Colleen leaned over the bed. "Do you know what happened to you?"

Craig looked at her and shook his head slowly.

"Your car exploded on the highway. A news team for a TV station was nearby and filmed most of it."

Craig stared at her. His lips moved. She leaned closer. He whispered: "Car accident?"

She stood away from the bed and shook her head. "It wasn't any accident," she said. "Somebody tried to kill you."

Craig said slowly: "Why are you here?"

"If you're going to stay alive," she said, "I think you're going to need me."

In 1947 Julius Stearns was in Las Vegas going over the books of the Flamingo Hotel Casino shortly after it opened. Meyer Lansky was in the process of ousting his longtime friend and syndicate partner, Bugsy Siegel. Siegel had come up with the idea of establishing a plush gambling center in the desert away from the downtown joints in Vegas. Through Lansky he had managed to borrow syndicate money to construct the Flamingo. The syndicate was pissed because Bugsy was looking for exclusive control of the desert operations.

When the Flamingo failed, closed, and then reopened later but was clearing only a fraction of what the syndicate was expecting, Bugsy decided to skip the country with a half-million dollars of syndicate money.

Lansky got an inkling of what was going on and came to Vegas to try to persuade Bugsy to adopt a different course of action. They holed up in a hotel room for several hours, and when Lansky came out of the room looking grim, he put out a contract on his friend.

Bugsy was shot and killed a few days later.

When it was all over Lansky confided to Julius what had happened in the room. Bugsy had changed his mind about going to Europe. The Flamingo, he was convinced, was going to make it, and he saw himself, in his arrogance, running the whole show—without the syndicate, and without Lansky.

Meyer said he had no choice.

Talking to Frank on the phone again, Julius was reminded of that conversation with Meyer. Your friend goes astray, and in the world they inhabited then you had no choice but to have him hit. It was quite simple then and no one questioned it.

Now, Frank Bishop was saying, "I tell you, Julie, I've got no choice. The guy killed my son. I let him get away with it, what the hell are they going to say about Frank Bishop? He's lost his nerve? He can't run things anymore? Julie, you know better than that. It's not how this business works."

"You go ahead with this," Julius said, "and you're going to have a war on your hands. A family war."

"You mean Colleen?"

"I mean Colleen."

Frank was silent. Julius let him think about it. "I can't help that," Frank said. Silence bothered him; he was a man of action. "She wouldn't even come up here to her brother's funeral. She got the hots for this guy or what?"

"She doesn't believe he killed Carl. She thinks

you're setting him up because of some old-fashioned pride, a vendetta killing, Frank, she won't go along with it."

"Colleen's not running this place. I've tried to keep her out of the business, you know that, but I can't let the guy walk over me. I've got no choice. What choice have I got? You tell me."

"Frank, life isn't so simple anymore. You can't go around taking people out just because things go wrong. Too many things go wrong these days, stuff doesn't work. The phone company fucks you over, what are you going to do, go down and shoot everybody in the place because Frank Bishop doesn't take any shit? It isn't like the old days, Frank."

"Don't lecture me, Julie. What do you know? You were never a participant in life, anyway. You were more like a peeping Tom. You had a good head for numbers, but you sat back in an office someplace and did your books. You were never out there calling the shots. Guys like Meyer and me had to make the tough calls."

Julius felt like banging the receiver down on the old fool. "What is this crap, Frank? You sound like a politician running for office. You're too old for this. Take a break."

"Don't swear at me, Julie. And just tell me one thing. Are you in or out?"

"In or out of what?"

"With me or against me?"

"Stop this nonsense, Frank. All I'm doing is trying to protect Colleen."

"That's your decision, then. So you're against me. Dear God, Julie, what's going to become of us?"

Colleen visited Craig Chappell in the hospital each day. She talked to him, found out more about him. In less than a week the swelling in his lip was down and he was able to talk more easily.

The police had also been there, questioned him and told him they'd found traces of a bomb that appeared to have been wired into his odometer, in effect creating a timing mechanism. They wanted to know if he had any idea who might have wanted to kill him. Craig told them he couldn't think of anyone offhand. But in his line of work you never knew. The police wanted a list of any suspects. He said he'd work on one.

"Why didn't you tell them about Frank and John Brown?" Colleen asked when he told her about the police visit.

Craig just shrugged and looked away.

"This is something personal now, isn't it? Between you and Brown?"

"It's always been personal."

"Men," Colleen said. "Listen, you need all the help you can get. You're going to be lucky to walk out of this hospital alive. If I were you and somebody walked in this room I didn't know, I think I'd have my hand on the call buzzer."

"Thanks," Craig said. "What would I do without you?"

"You still don't get it, do you? You think this is all some joke."

"I don't know what it is. And I can't figure you out."

"Why try?"

"I'm not used to people taking such an interest in my life," Craig said. "Why are you doing it?"

"I told you. I don't want to see you hurt."

"I appreciate your concern. But believe me, I can take care of myself."

Colleen stared at him and smiled. "You look like a guy who can take care of himself," she said.

123

John Leslie

She watched him laugh, as much as he could laugh, and laughed with him. For the next few days they began to talk. About themselves, who they were, or thought they were, and what was going on in their lives. She told him about the incident with Frank when she was a kid. Something she'd never talked about with anyone ever until she'd told the young intern at the hospital. And she told him about her attempt to kill herself.

It all came out naturally, like she had it under control, in perspective, and she didn't feel embarrassed talking about it. It had happened; it was part of her past, and it couldn't hurt her anymore. Craig was a good listener, and he was much nicer than she had at first thought. She had seen him as a macho, not much different from some of the thugs who hung around Frank. But that wasn't the case. He was more complicated than that.

"Have you ever been married?" she asked him.

"Once, a long time ago," he said. "Why?"

"I was just wondering. You're not the tough guy you like to pretend you are."

"You're not seeing me at my best," he said.

She smiled. "Maybe I will someday . . . if you start taking better care of yourself."

"I intend to. As soon as I get out of here and deal with the asshole who was responsible for this."

"Now you're back to being macho," she said. "You wear a lot of disguises."

"And you're too smart for your own good."

Colleen said, "Frank says that too."

_____ ***Thirteen***

HE SPENT MOST OF THE AFTERNOON ON THE PHONE setting up the swap.

What was it now, nine months he'd been out? It was funny, guys sit in prison and can tell you down to the minute practically how much time they've done. On the outside you forget where you were a week ago. So much going on, you don't even think about time. Inside he had missed that action, twenty years of not doing anything but prison routine. Finally, he was getting back into the groove.

At four-thirty that afternoon he left the hotel,

carrying his briefcase; he'd taken out the nine-millimeter and carried it inside his waistband, wearing his suit jacket. Outside he hailed a cab. And told the driver, "The Fontainebleau," saying it Fountain Blue.

It had been Sly's choice. He could have gone to the airport or the bus depot, but he'd finally settled on a big hotel. He wanted someplace large and public where a couple of guys with bags wouldn't be noticed —but not too unnoticed, Sly thought. The tricky part was going to be when they had to open the bags, check the contents, make sure nobody was being cheated. Like sacks full of baking soda in the bag he was going to get, for example; the other guy wanting to make sure that under the top hundred-dollar bill the rest wasn't play money.

Sly thought he had a good plan.

Brown was across the street from the hotel, having a *buchi* in a little Cuban coffee place, when Sly came out. Brown had to sprint but he made his car, which was parked at a meter, before Gallanti was able to find a free cab. Where the fuck's he going now? Brown wondered, pulling away from the curb. He was tired of hanging around and irritable after drinking the strong Cuban coffee all afternoon.

They didn't go far. Up to the Fontainebleau, where Brown had to park in a no-parking zone to be able to keep Gallanti in sight, watching as the old man paid off the cab and went into the hotel. Brown followed across the huge lobby, trying to appear casual, stopping to buy a newspaper from a vending machine, turning as he did so he wouldn't lose Gallanti.

Something was going on here, Brown could feel it.

He followed him downstairs past the fancy indoor

shops surrounded by glass windows. It was like a
carnival, running around bumping into yourself, or a
small town, everything you wanted in one building.
Except the swamp, Brown thought. You didn't get the
swamp in here.

Gallanti went into the restaurant, nothing formal,
more like a big coffee shop that must have been able to
seat two hundred people. And not more than ten
people scattered around the place. Brown thought of
another cup of coffee and began to tremble. He
ducked into one of the shops, women's swim wear,
from where he had a view inside the restaurant, which
was also enclosed in glass.

Brown browsed through the women's clothes, some
excitement building as he ran his hands over the
garments, looking inside the bikini bottoms at the
white cloth padding that would rest snug against their
pusses. He could see them: some of the pusses had
been shaved so all that hair was tucked inside that
little patch of cloth, maybe just some prickles showing, like pimples, on that tender skin where the leg and
the groin met. Then there were women who just let it
all hang out, hair growing wild around the edges of the
bikini. He couldn't imagine any women around the
Fontainebleau who would appear like that, though.

"May I help you?"

"Huh? Oh, no. Just looking for something for my
wife." He hadn't seen her sneak up on him like that.

"You know her size?" Smiling like she'd caught him
in the act.

"'Bout your size. I find something, maybe you'd
model it for me. See how it looks," Brown said.
Smiling right back at her.

"I can't do that," she said, the smile gone now. "But
if you need any other help I'll be right here."

"I'll just look around then," Brown said. "I find something, I'll bring the wife in." The girl nodded and walked away.

He looked through the glass into the restaurant. Gallanti was seated at a table in back, away from anyone. His briefcase was on the table. Brown moved around to the hanging, traditional swimsuits, from where he had a better view of Gallanti. And watched as another man joined Gallanti at the table. The guy was carrying one of those shiny aluminum cases that looked like a small oversized suitcase. Which went on top of the table too. Half the size of a suitcase, but bigger than the briefcase.

A waitress came, took their order, went away and returned seconds later with two cups of coffee. Brown shuddered.

When she was gone Gallanti and the other guy opened their cases. Like a couple of lawyers about to go over papers. But no papers came out. Brown didn't expect them to. He had a good idea now what was going on, watching as Gallanti examined the contents of the other case, poking a finger, removing it and putting it in his mouth like he was sampling candy. Jesus, it was wild. Right out in the open. The other guy looked in Gallanti's case, seemed satisfied, and the covers were closed. They sipped their coffee for a moment. Then Gallanti stood up, shook hands and picked up the aluminum case, as Brown knew he would.

Leaving the other man sitting there with the briefcase Gallanti had carried in.

Brown hurried out of the shop, well ahead of Gallanti, and walked up the stairs to the lobby, glancing once over his shoulder to see that the old man was there, walking in the same direction.

Brown went out to his car, found a ticket beneath

128

the windshield wiper (at least it wasn't towed away) and got in to wait for Gallanti to come out and get a cab. Which he did.

And Brown followed the cab back to the garage where Gallanti went in with his shiny aluminum case, and then moments later came back to the waiting cab empty-handed.

Thinking about it later, Brown decided he should have stayed with the guy who got Gallanti's case. That was the prize. No, what he should have done was put the .45 in Gallanti's back when he first thought about it, when Gallanti left the garage earlier today, and then he would have had the briefcase. But he was supposed to be working for Frank, right? Sort of, he guessed. Right now he felt like working for himself.

He decided to stick with the old man and see where else he went. Which was when things began to get very interesting.

Biscayne Boulevard near the park. Sly sat on a park bench and watched the evening street traffic begin to form. Some of these kids no more than eighteen, nineteen years old would hustle for five, ten bucks. Or crack. Crack, a cheap high from rock cocaine, was the big thing now. Some of these characters would go down on a dead buzzard for crack.

Sly wore a short-sleeved shirt with leaping dolphins printed on it, his thin arms beginning to tan, making him, he thought, a younger, more attractive mark.

To punks like the one he saw now. The kid couldn't be over twenty; although next year you'd never know it—the kid would look forty if he were still alive.

From his park bench Sly said, "You want to get high?"

The kid looked. Sly flashed a small bag of rock he'd taken from his shirt pocket. The kid stopped, a tough street stance, the legs apart, a cigarette hanging from one hand. He said, "You wanna blow me, it's gonna cost you a couple rocks."

"What's your name?" Sly asked.

"Kenny."

"Kenny, let's not have an argument. We just met. You want three rocks, they're yours. But you've got to change your thinking. You got the action backwards."

Kenny said, "Come on, pop." Sly got up and followed as Kenny left the sidewalk and cut across the grass to some bushes behind the library. They were off the path, out of sight.

"Give me the rock," Kenny said. He had picked up a diet Coke can that had been stashed in the bushes.

Sly took out the bag, opened it and handed him one rock. Kenny dusted cigarette ash over some punctured holes in the Coke can, then put the crack on top of that. Putting his mouth over the opening in the top of the can, he held a match to the rock, sucked in the smoke and held it.

Sly unzipped, waiting, as Kenny smoked the stuff down to nothing. When Kenny looked up, his face was red, contorted, his eyes narrowed to dark points of hatred; his hands trembled as he dropped the Coke can back into the bushes and straightened up, hooking a leg behind Sly's and with a forearm shoving Sly in the chest.

Sly fell back into the shrubs. Kenny was on him, had him by the throat. Kenny said, "Fuck you, pop," in a different tone of voice than the way he'd been talking just moments ago. "Give me the fuckin' rock or I'll squeeze your brains out through your ears."

He knew the kid, even wasted, was still too young, too strong to fight off. He wished he hadn't left the nine-millimeter in his hotel room. Kenny squeezed harder, raising Sly's head, the stiff branches scratching against his head and face. He couldn't breathe. Kenny had his knee in Sly's chest, pinning the old man's left hand there. Sly tried to reach his other hand into his shirt pocket for the bag of crack.

"Let him go, scumbag."

Sly heard the voice, tried to look over Kenny's shoulder. He felt Kenny ease up on his throat, and Sly turned his head. The guy was standing there, holding a gun against the back of Kenny's head. Kenny said, "All right, man, all right. I wasn't going to hurt him." His other voice back now, the kid voice, as he stood up.

"I know you wasn't because I been watchin' you. Now vamoose before I get pissed and blow you away." Kenny took off running across the grass, back toward Biscayne Boulevard.

Sly sat up, brushing himself, feeling his head for any serious wounds. A little blood, but just surface scratches. He looked up at the guy standing there, holding the gun down at his side now. Sly rubbed his throat. "Thanks," he said. He got to his feet.

"Jesus, you a little old for this, ain'tcha, old-timer? Out for a stroll in the park, thought you might get your ashes hauled, is that it?"

Sly said, "The kid got crazy on that shit."

"Some of 'em do that. This ain't an area you want ·to hang out in after dark."

Sly tested his legs. The guy tucked the gun in the waistband of his pants and let the squared-off shirttail drop over his waist. "I'll walk you out of here. Where do you live?"

"South Beach," Sly said.

"Hey, I'm going that way myself. I'll drop you off."

Sly wasn't sure. He could just get a cab, not put the man out. He wasn't being put out, the man said. Going that way anyway. Sly wanted to go home, take a shower. Get into bed. It had been a long day. He didn't need any more trouble. But he followed the guy to his car on Biscayne and got in; there was something familiar about the car. When they crossed the MacArthur Causeway into South Beach, Sly felt better.

"I'm up on Collins," Sly said.

"Yeah, I got a stop to make first, though."

Sly wasn't sure where they were, trying to get his bearings, see some landmarks, finally recognizing the street they were on as being the one where the garage was. The bus. The garage coming up, in fact, in the next block, the guy slowing down like he was looking for something, then stopping right in front of the garage. The bus was parked outside, behind a locked fence.

Sly knew now why the car had seemed familiar: he'd seen it a couple times today, an ordinary car like any other car—he couldn't tell one make from the other anymore, but yeah, this one had definitely crossed his path today. Maybe he was too old for this shit. Been fooling himself all this time thinking he could step back in after twenty years and take up where he'd left off. Think people were supposed to know Sly Gallanti, and respect him.

"What is this?" Sly said.

"Mr. Gallanti, I think maybe we ought to check the product, be sure everything's all right," John Brown said.

Fourteen

ON SATURDAY, AFTER A WEEK IN JACKSON MEMORIAL,
Craig was released from the hospital. Still bruised and
sore, with his arm in a half-cast supported by a blue
canvas sling, he hobbled out, found a cab in front and
took his time getting into the backseat; his body
wasn't going to be quick to let him forget the abuse it
had taken. After giving the cabbie directions for
taking him home, Craig sat back and looked out the
open window. Miami's traffic, the noise, its humid air
hit him for the first time with pleasure. Pure and
simple pleasure. He was alive.

He thought about Colleen Bishop. There was something about her that kept him thinking about her. She was so goddamn persistent, was part of it, but there was something else, something he couldn't put his finger on. He'd met people before who just opened up to you, began telling you their life story, the most intimate details, when you hadn't even asked to hear it. Showing you how friendly they were, and then the next thing, they wanted to borrow your car, get you to invest in a little business they had going that was a sure winner. And sometimes all they really wanted was to talk.

But Colleen wasn't like that. She didn't just want to talk, and she wasn't trying to con him into anything. She was frightened and lonely. And that strong front she put up was just that, he thought—a front. She probably was concerned about his safety too, but it was more than that. It was like he'd given her something in New York, information about himself, personal stuff, the business about Barry, Craig's attachment to his brother, everything. It was like she was repaying him, coming into the hospital every day, talking about her own life, telling him all that stuff.

He liked her too. She was different. Not the sort of spoiled, pouty chick he was used to, the ones somebody had once told they were cute and they'd never forgotten it. Colleen Bishop had something: it was the ability to look at a person in a situation and sum it up, get right to the heart of the problem, see through the veneer of personality. She would have been great at tracking down skips.

As the cab stopped at a light on Le Jeune Road, the driver turned in his seat, a Latin wearing a mesh bill cap that said: MIAMI NICE. Probably from that school they had a couple years ago where they taught cab drivers how to get tips and sell Miami at the same time, Craig thought. Unfortunately they didn't teach them how to stay alive when some crack addict with a gun was in the backseat looking for a few dollars to get him high.

The cabbie said, "Boy, going to get up there today. Your first day out, right? Must feel pretty good."

Craig said yeah, it felt good.

"The snowbirds will be loving this weather." The cabbie grinned and turned back as the light changed, working on his tip.

When they got to Kendall and the cab pulled into his driveway, Craig told the driver to keep the meter running, he'd be right out. He went in, changed clothes, pulled on a lightweight sport jacket and tucked the .38 in the outside pocket before going out to get into the waiting cab.

All that thinking about Colleen Bishop brought back to him what he'd been going to do before the accident. He didn't see any reason to change his plans now, and the idea of laying around the house waiting for his body to heal seemed like wasted time. He might as well get to work; now was as good a time as any.

"We're going to go over to Biscayne Boulevard," Craig told the cabbie. "Near the Holiday Inn. I'll show you when we get there."

Jeannie Exeter lived in one of the older condos along the boulevard. He'd been in her apartment once, when he put the wiretap on her phone. It seemed like years ago. And it seemed like the place to start if he were going to find John Brown.

When they got to the condo, Craig had the driver stop in front. He gave him a twenty and told him to keep the meter running; he'd be out soon.

There was a bank of buttons outside the door, next to the names of the tenants. The last time he'd pushed

Jeannie's buzzer, when he brought the bug in, he knew she wouldn't be there. She was working the Omni lounge that afternoon. Still, he'd played it cautious. When there was no answer he punched some buzzers for other apartments until someone answered, then he had said, "Federal Express." He'd been buzzed in, went directly to Jeannie's apartment and picked the lock.

This time he buzzed Jeannie, and heard her familiar voice, not quite so breathy as he remembered it.

"I've got a message for John Brown," Craig said.

"Just a minute," Jeannie said. Like the guy was sitting in her living room and she'd gone to get him. Craig began wondering if he'd made the right move.

John Brown was shaving, standing naked in front of the sink-to-ceiling bathroom mirror, thinking about Jeannie with the light brown hair, the thick bush that grew in an almost perfect triangle between her legs. Thinking about it gave him half a hard-on which he could watch grow in the mirror. He'd walk out of the bathroom like this and tackle her, watch her face as she looked from him to his cock, first smiling, then serious, and then pouty as they headed for the bedroom; or he'd take her right there, bending over the sink.

He was thinking about that. And he was thinking about the aluminum case that was in the bedroom, filled with sacks of cocaine, when she knocked on the door. He reached over and pulled it open. And saw her standing there looking from his face to his cock and then begin laughing. "You playing with yourself?"

"I was thinking about you," Brown said.

"Well, you better stop thinking about me. There's a guy downstairs says he has a message for you."

Brown felt himself droop. As far as he knew, no one

except Frank and Jeannie knew he was here. The only person who might have had suspicions was the bounty hunter, Craig Chappell, who had lived through the car bomb. But the guy would have to have lead balls to come here and ask for him.

"What's he doing?"

"I told him to wait a minute."

"You say I was here?"

"No."

Brown thought quickly. He didn't want a confrontation here with Jeannie watching. If it was Chappell, the guy wasn't paying a social call.

When Brown returned to Miami and found the bug in the phone, confirming his earlier suspicions, he imagined Chappell sitting there listening as he and Jeannie had some long distance sex. That was the night the first Chappell showed up—Barry, Chappell One, the younger brother. He imagined Craig sitting there listening, getting off maybe, and later realizing what had happened: that standing outside in the hall, with a pair of cuffs in his hand, was Barry.

Which meant this was no longer just a job to Chappell—it was a grudge match. There would be no fair fight, just shoot now, ask questions later.

"Okay," Brown told Jeannie, "let him in but don't say I'm here. I'll be in the bedroom. Find out what he wants. I'll be able to hear you. If there's any trouble I'll come out. If I don't, get rid of him."

Jeannie smiled, backing out the door. "Don't go blind playing with yourself," she said.

After Jeannie buzzed him in, Craig rode the elevator up to the sixth floor, wondering what he was walking into. She'd left him standing outside for fifty seconds—he'd timed her—long enough to get whoever was in there with her out, or at least warned. So

137

what was he doing, walking straight into a trap, repeating Barry's mistake? Craig couldn't believe that Brown, if he was here, would try anything with Jeannie and a condo full of neighbors around. For all Brown knew, he had a SWAT team with him.

No, it was more likely that he and Brown would size each other up, get this thing out in the open, Craig decided, coming off the elevator and walking down the corridor to the apartment. Then, the next time they met they could go for their guns, walking down the street, Biscayne Boulevard, stopping traffic; or maybe the beach, all the tourists watching them, thinking they were making a movie.

He had to stop that—that kind of thinking was the way you got killed. But it was the way he wanted Brown. Just the two of them. Alone. He cleared his mind and began to think about nothing except staying alive. Then walked up to the door and knocked.

Jeannie opened it. Smiled, and asked him in. He saw her lying on the bed, naked, playing with herself while Brown gave her directions over the phone. He also saw into the room behind her. He pushed the door all the way open as he crossed the threshold to make sure there was no one behind it. There was a lot of modern Italian plastic furniture, a combined living room/dining room, and an L-shaped kitchen separated from the dining room by swing doors. There was a hallway that probably led to the bedrooms and bath. If Brown were here, he'd be back there, Craig guessed. From where he stood he could see that the doors were closed along the hallway.

Craig walked over and stood by the window that looked out over Miami's skyline. In the distance he could see the harbor.

He turned and looked back at Jeannie. She was

138

standing in the center of the room, wearing shorts and a man's striped button-down dress shirt, the sleeves rolled up above her elbows, the collar unbuttoned, turned up around her neck. He stared at her.

"I kind of like the view from here," he said. "I never thought I would, the way these places block off the water, but they're not bad buildings, are they?"

"What are you, in real estate? Do you go around checking people's apartments for the view? This one isn't for sale."

"No. I look for people. What took you so long to let me in, Jeannie?"

She cocked her head slightly. "I was running a bath. I didn't want it to run over."

"Took you almost a minute to turn off a faucet in a small place like this?"

She looked at him like he was crazy. And moved around to the doorway leading down the hall. "What do you want?" she asked. Getting aggressive now.

"Your boyfriend. Is he here?" Craig was aware of performing, getting back into the role he always played in these circumstances. Determined but quiet, letting them know he was on the edge of being a kick-ass dude. He hadn't known until he got in here just how this was going to play. A moment ago he thought he might storm the place, bang open a few doors, check the rooms—look in the bathroom and he'd bet he'd find a dry tub. He would scare the shit out of Jeannie, but he could do that just talking to her, without taking the chance of getting his head blown off.

"Maybe I should call the cops. How'd you know my name?"

"Call them," Craig said. "I'll dial 911 for you. But you might want to remember a long distance call John

139

Brown, a felon at the time, made to you from Montreal a few weeks ago. He woke you up, got you a little excited. Remember?"

He watched her blush, turn her head coylike to the side, away from him. Obviously not knowing her phone had been tapped. Brown must have removed the bug when he got back here without telling her anything about it. The line had gone dead about a week ago.

"You sonofabitch," she said.

"Careful, lady. Brown killed my brother. I just got out of the hospital after your boyfriend wired a bomb to my car. I'm not feeling too generous right now. You wouldn't want me to start shooting the place up, would you?"

She stared at him, looking him in the eyes now. "I don't know who you are," she said, "but I want you to leave."

"You didn't even ask me the message I had for Brown."

She didn't move from the doorway. Craig walked to the front door. "It's all right," he said. "I can understand your not being too curious, living with that animal. But tell him I'm going to kill him. Just him and me. No cops. Tell him I'll get a nice quiet spot for us and I'll be in touch."

Jeannie came into the bedroom. Brown was lying on the bed, naked, the .45 on the pillow next to him. For a while now he'd been thinking about dumping Jeannie; she was beginning to bore him. But seeing her come in the bedroom, her face serious, upset, not even looking down at the hard-on he'd worked up for her, he knew the asshole had scared her. Chappell had made a threat against her man, and Brown sensed her fear. A sudden rush of tenderness came over him.

"Did you hear what he said?" Jeannie asked.

"He said he was going to kill me," Brown said. The threat amused him; listening through the cracked door to Chappell, he had started formulating a plan for dealing with the asshole bounty hunter.

"Before that," Jeannie said.

The feeling of tenderness was gone. He tried to think what else Chappell had said that would upset her. "What'd he say?" Brown asked.

"He said he heard us."

"Heard us?"

Jeannie stared at him in disbelief. "Heard us doing it on the phone," she said. "He was listening."

Women, Brown thought. Who could figure them out, what was going to get them riled? "So what?" he said, miffed now that she wasn't more concerned about his well-being.

"So what?" Her voice rose an octave. "Did you know he was listening?"

"I figured it out later."

"What are you going to do about it?"

"I've already done it. I took the bug off the phone."

"And that's it? The guy listens to a very intimate conversation and then comes into my home and tells me about it. Embarrassing me. And you've done all you're going to do?"

"Maybe not everything. You're cute when you get mad. Come on over here. I'll tell you what else I'm going to do."

"I don't like guns," Jeannie said. She was calming down now.

"Hey," Brown said. "How 'bout this one?" Reaching down. "See if it's got six shots in it."

The two-bedroom frame bungalow in Kendall where Craig Chappell lived had at one time been part

141

of the first of the small-tract developments in the suburbs, mushrooming into a major residential area over the years. Craig had added a screened-in Florida Room and enclosed the carport to make storage space for the boating and fishing gear he had accumulated.

The neighborhood was quiet at four o'clock in the morning. The third night home Craig lay half awake, still feeling the pain from his injuries but refusing to take the prescribed painkillers. That stuff knocked you out for eight hours. You didn't feel any pain, all right, but Jesus, you might as well be dead.

After the confrontation with Jeannie, he was thinking it might be in his best interests to stay alert, even if it meant some pain and loss of sleep.

He was thinking about getting up and swallowing a couple of aspirin when he heard what sounded like a bottle breaking. And then another one hit the picture window in the living room with a loud ka-ploom and a crash of glass. He could hear and feel the heat from the fire that was burning in the living room.

He got to his feet, made his way along the hall which was filling with smoke, down to the Florida Room and out into the small fenced-in backyard.

Moments later he watched—glad now he hadn't stopped to take anything—as the whole house went up in a curtain of flames. Thinking, if anybody bothered later to sift through the rubble, they'd find enough evidence to prove that the fire had started when someone tossed a homemade bomb through the window. The sort of thing kids threw at buildings and cars and each other in Lebanon.

But the kids of Kendall, Craig knew, hadn't taken up guerrilla warfare.

Fifteen

T HERE WAS THAT ONE TIME WHEN HE'D LEFT NEW JER-
sey and come to Florida. Giving up everything that
was familiar then, a job with the Newark police, his
family, Barry and his mom and dad, to come down
here and start over. He had a wife, but she was new
too. There was a sense of adventure about the move,
and even though it was a gamble, he knew he could
always go back to Newark if it didn't pan out. The
cops had given him a going-away party, told him, Hey,
how many white cops were there in Newark anyway?
Joking. The black brothers saying, Yeah, you get tired

of all that sunshine, we take you back. You a minority, we don't discriminate, this a equal opportunity employer.

Craig wondered what they'd say now, he showed back up in Newark after all these years? He wouldn't know anybody, that was for sure. Well, he wasn't thinking of doing that anyway, but this was really starting over. You get to forty, you were supposed to be settling down, getting into stride, not going through this shit.

He stood outside watching his life literally go up in smoke. He had on a pair of sweat pants that he'd been sleeping in, and he'd grabbed a shirt when he raced outside, and the pants that had his wallet in the pocket. So he stood there with everything he owned, watching the firemen put out the blaze. Neighbors up and down the street had come out. There was the noise of police and fire radios, flashing lights. The street was soaked where the big canvas hoses lay like swollen snakes.

Craig didn't pay any attention to it. He just stood there with the rest of the crowd in the predawn darkness watching as the fire was put out, seeing it but still not believing it, the reality of it, that he was starting life over again, and he didn't have a damn thing to show for the last forty years except what he had on his back. The rest was history.

He had some emergency cash that he kept in a small safe at the office. You never knew when you were going to need some money in this business on a day when the banks were closed. Craig still had his credit cards; he could get himself some clothes and necessities. He could sack out in the office here until he figured out what he was going to do next.

He waited until eight o'clock in the morning, which

seemed like a reasonable hour, before calling Colleen Bishop.

"If this were the Winter Olympics I'd have a medal for the fastest time in the downhill run," Craig said when she answered.

"What's happened now?"

"My house was torched last night."

Colleen was silent.

"About four o'clock this morning," Craig went on. "Lucky I wasn't able to sleep. Otherwise I wouldn't be telling you about it."

"How much more of this are you willing to go through?" She sounded mad, or maybe just exasperated. It was hard to tell.

"Last week I lost my car, this week my house . . ."

"And before that your brother. What are you going to do?"

"You got any suggestions?" Craig asked.

"Maybe," Colleen said. "Meet me at my hotel at noon, if you can make it."

"I got a busy schedule but I'll try to fit you in."

"Just try to stay alive," Colleen said.

After breakfast she walked down to the C-Breeze. Julius was on the porch reading the *Miami Herald.*

"You see this?" he asked Colleen when she came up.

"What is it?"

"I can't believe this stuff. You ever see so many kids with medical problems? All these transplants. They got five-, six-year-old kids looking for new kidneys, livers, hearts. What's wrong with them? I never heard of so many kids with these conditions. What did they do before transplants?"

"They died," Colleen said. "You didn't hear about that."

"All these American kids?" Julius sounded out-

145

raged. Like he couldn't believe American kids ever had medical problems. "They're being born with defective organs. What's going on in this country?"

Colleen pulled a chair over close to Julius. She smiled at the old woman who was setting up a checkerboard on a low table.

"You had it right before," Colleen said. "It's medical science at work. A lot of publicity for a few doctors around the country experimenting with organ transplants."

"You see the money the parents are raising. Half a million dollars pouring in to this one kid's family, and they haven't even found a kidney for him yet."

"What are you saying? Do you think it's a scam?" she asked.

"I don't know. If it is, the mother's got to be hard as nails."

Colleen leaned back in her chair. Julius was loosely folding the newspaper, dropping it on the porch. "I want you to meet someone," Colleen said.

"Who's that?"

"Craig Chappell. The guy Frank thinks killed Carl."

"Him? I thought you were going to forget about him."

"I can't forget about him," she said. "Not as long as Frank is trying to have him killed."

"Colleen, we went through this once before. Don't get mixed up in this."

"I already am," she said. "The guy's lost everything. His car a week ago. He just got out of the hospital and somebody firebombed his house."

"Frank, you think?"

"Julius, you know it as well as I do. Frank's put out a contract on Craig Chappell."

"What do you want me to do?"

"Meet him. Just talk to him."

"You trying to set something up? If Frank knew you were doing this he'd have contracts out on both of us."

"I'm not going to stand by and watch that guy get killed," Colleen said.

Julius shook his head. "I can't believe I'm doing this. The guy's some sort of cop, isn't he?"

Colleen said. "Chappell Security, Inc. He's a recovery agent, a skip tracer; those are the fancy terms he told me for what he does."

"A bounty hunter. And you want to get me involved?"

"Julius, you wanted me to come down here because you needed my help. Now I need yours."

"Boy, oh, boy. I don't like this. You're getting into something you aren't going to be able to handle."

Colleen smiled. "At least I'm not running a scam."

He couldn't believe it. Sitting here on a porch with all these old people. The guy talking, Colleen's friend, who had once worked for Meyer Lansky. Who would have believed it? Craig wasn't sure what this was all about. Colleen said she wanted him to meet Julius, so they had walked down here from her hotel. Julius stared at him, shook his hand, his left hand, staring at Craig's right hand in the cast and blue sling when Colleen introduced them.

"Colleen says you been having some problems."

This was the part he didn't get. He understood Colleen wanted to help him, was afraid for him. Jesus, after last night he had to admit he could use all the help he could get. But he couldn't figure out what this old man was supposed to be able to do for him. From the looks of Julius, he was having similar thoughts.

"It's been one of those months." Craig smiled. Julius didn't even look at him, giving nothing away.

"You expect it to get better?"

"It can't get any worse."

"I wouldn't bet on it."

Craig looked at Colleen. The three of them sat facing the ocean. It was awkward, but Colleen seemed to be at ease. It was like some kind of weird stage set, all these old people sitting facing the ocean, the same show playing day in, day out. It seemed like there was a message here, but Craig wondered if anybody was getting it.

"I tried to tell him the same thing," Colleen said after a stubborn silence.

"The trouble is," Craig said, "you all have got the inside track in some kind of family deal. I keep getting told about the danger, but what am I supposed to do?"

"I don't know," Julius said. "It's a good question. Colleen, this was your idea, you got any answers?"

"Yes," Colleen said, "I do. We take him in, protect him until Frank can be convinced to stop this."

Julius let his head drop forward, his chin resting against his chest. Craig was afraid he'd gone to sleep. He could hardly blame him.

"Don't worry about me," Craig said. He was beginning to feel like a charity case. "I'll be able to look after myself."

Julius lifted his head. "No, you won't," he said.

What the hell was he supposed to do? First Colleen, and now Julius, telling him he couldn't take care of himself. The almighty Frank Bishop was just too powerful. Everybody kept telling him he didn't have a chance, but nobody had any suggestions. Craig said that, said he was tired of being told he couldn't take care of himself, and he was more tired of being one of Frank Bishop's victims. And since all anybody seemed to want to do was to keep telling him how much danger he was in without coming up with any ideas for dealing with it, he should just go, stop wasting everybody's time.

"Where will you go?" Colleen asked.

"The first thing is to find a place to live."

"And wait for John Brown to strike again," Colleen said.

"I'll take care of Brown."

Julius turned toward him, looked at Craig for the first time since he'd sat down. "You're not paying attention to what she's been telling you. It isn't just Brown. There are hundreds like him. Frank can put his finger on any one of them. You don't have a chance."

"The best thing I think is for him to check into my hotel," Colleen said, talking now to Julius, like Craig wasn't even there. "I can keep an eye on him until something better comes along."

"I want to talk to a guy," Julius said. "Maybe the something better is sitting around the corner right now."

"I don't get it," Craig said. "Would somebody mind telling me why you're doing this?"

"Talk to Colleen," Julius said. "This is her idea."

He went back to the Carlyle with her and was told they were full. So he'd stay in his office, or find another hotel.

"No," Colleen said. "You can stay with me. There are two beds in the room." She looked up at him, serious, no smile. "I'm not coming on to you," she said. "I'm offering you a place to sleep."

Why not? It was better than being alone. She smiled and offered to go with him to buy some things he would need, a few clothes.

Still trying to figure her out, he walked with her up

149

Collins Avenue and turned off on Twelfth Street, looking for some department stores. As they walked, Craig said, "Julius would do anything for you, wouldn't he?"

"He's always been like that with me. I've known him since I was a kid," Colleen said. "He was more like a father to me than Frank."

"And he's willing to go up against Frank for somebody he doesn't even know just on your say so?"

"You heard him. He'll figure something out. He's getting old. It makes him feel useful."

"I thought he was writing a book."

"I'm doing the writing. He's giving me the material. Maybe he feels like he owes me something."

"That explains Julius. Now what about you? Who do you owe?"

"You wouldn't believe me if I told you."

"Try me."

Colleen gave him a look as he held the door for her going into the store. Walking down the aisle between stacks of brightly colored folded shirts, she said, "I think I've always wanted to get even with Frank Bishop, maybe for what I told you in the hospital the other day. And maybe for more stuff I don't even know about yet. So if you need reasons, why don't you just think of me as using you. To find out about myself."

Somehow he didn't have a problem with that: Colleen Bishop using Craig Chappell. Bishop and Chappell. They sounded like a corny Sunday morning religious service on TV. But in the crazy world he was living in, it made some kind of sense. He didn't ask her any more questions.

"I been here a couple of weeks and I'm ready to get out of this town," Sly Gallanti said.

"You get used to it," Julius said. "Times are different."

"There's no respect here. People are crazy," Gallanti said. "A bunch of cons, ripoff artists. Kids too. You think there'd be a little more respect for the elderly."

"Sly, what happened? Somebody rip you off?" Julius had worried about Sly, how he was going to make it here, anywhere, after twenty years inside. Times were different. A guy like Sly wasn't going to have it easy adjusting.

"Look," Sly said. "I had a promising thing going. Frank put up a hundred grand. I was gonna move some product going back up to New York. It was a cinch."

"What kind of product?"

"The stuff that's in demand right now."

"Coke."

"A suitcase full of it mixed in with the old people's bags going back on the bus. A simple ride. You got little risk. It moves fast and pays big."

"That's what Colleen was talking about the other day."

"Yeah, she'd picked up on it. But it's all off now. I got mugged in the goddamn park over on Biscayne by some riffraff scum, a kid I got high. This guy came along and probably saved my life, then he drove me straight to the fuckin' bus where I'd stored the product earlier in the day. It was like the whole thing was set up."

"Jesus Christ." Julius whistled.

"Frank's gonna shit," Sly said.

"Worse. Knowing Frank, he's going to think you're in on the scam."

"Fuck Frank."

"Yeah," Julius said. "I talked to a guy earlier tried

to do that. He's been ruined, he's starting life over, and I wouldn't give any odds that he'll see more than a week of this new one."

"So the only thing to do is get the product back."

"You have any place to begin?"

Sly shook his head.

Julius shrugged. "You pick up the paper and read where this kind of stuff goes on all the time down here. You're lucky you're still walking around. Most of them wind up in the river."

"You have any suggestions?" Sly asked.

"Yeah," Julius said, "stay out of the park."

_____ *Sixteen*

*T*HEY HAD DINNER IN THE RESTAURANT OF THE CAR-
lyle. A small combo played old jazz tunes, a lot of
Duke Ellington, some Count Basie, while tuxedoed
waiters slid quietly around the candlelit room. A man
at the table next to them was having dinner with a girl
who couldn't have been more than sixteen. She
seemed uncomfortable, maybe embarrassed, her head
bowed as she answered the man's questions.

"Dad on his weekly visit," Colleen whispered
across the table.

"Is that what it is?" Craig asked. "You're pretty

good at figuring out people and situations, aren't you?" The band held the final note on "Moon River," letting it fade slowly, and then jumped right into "Sophisticated Lady," no pause.

"I like watching people," she said. "I learn a lot."

Craig cut a piece of tender yellowtail with his fork and carried the fork up to his mouth in his left hand. He'd thought about ordering a steak. Colleen could cut it up in bite-size pieces for him. He liked watching her. "What are you going to do?" Craig asked, chewing the yellowtail. "I mean with what you learn? Are you going to write, or is this thing with Julius just play?"

Colleen sipped her wine, looking at him, not eating, her elbows on the table. "You know, I never thought about it. I study what I enjoy, but I don't know what I'll do with it. Maybe I will write."

"Teach?"

"No, definitely not."

"On the theory that those who can, do, and those who can't, teach?"

"I don't know about that," she said. "It sounds too pat. I just know I'd be bored."

She had a healthy look, her face and arms tanned, her hair sun-bleached but not dried out. In New York she had been pretty, but a lot of it was painted on. Here it was natural. He couldn't imagine her trying to kill herself. He said, "Can I ask you something?"

"Why not? We're going to be roommates. You already know I don't have any secrets."

"Why'd you do it? The suicide thing."

Colleen held the glass in both hands, examining the wine through candlelight. "I was tired, under a lot of stress," she said. "And I didn't like myself all that much, I guess."

"That sounds pat too."

She set her wineglass down. She said, "I'm not going to blame Frank, or my childhood. I'm twenty-two. I'm over it. I was depressed. You can't always find a reason for depression."

"You feeling better about yourself?"

She smiled. "Don't worry. I'm not going to OD on you, if that's what you're thinking."

"I'm not. Just trying to understand you."

"Do you want to psychoanalyze me? You already know a lot about me. I'll tell you what, you do me, I'll do you."

She was serious. A waiter poured wine. The guy at the next table was still absorbed in talking to the teenager who still sat with her head down. He leaned across the table, talking earnestly.

"All right, I'll go first," Colleen said. "You're a very stubborn person. You know what I think's wrong?"

This was kid stuff, Craig thought, but she seemed to be amused, and at least he wasn't sitting around by himself, brooding. "Go ahead, shoot," he said.

"Your wife left you years ago and you've never remarried. You have affairs once in a while but nothing ever lasting. I think you grew up with an idea about women that you've never been able to change. You expected too much from them. And when things didn't work out, you walked away. It seemed easier than trying to figure out what was going wrong. On to someone else. But never any commitment. Am I close?"

"I don't know, but don't let me stop you."

"You live in that male world where women are something to be used and replaced—like toys. They aren't part of that real world that you and your brother shared. A life and death world where you depended on each other for survival. It was a game and real at the same time, and you let your brother

155

down. You were to blame, and now you're going to spend the rest of your life feeling sorry for yourself. Nobody will be able to get close to you again."

"That's pretty good. I don't know if it's true, but it's pretty good."

"The difference between you and Frank, for example . . . well, you're nicer and you're not a criminal, but I'm sure you've got a lot of similar attitudes."

"Will you ever be able to forgive me?"

She smiled again. "There's nothing to forgive. You take people the way they come. You can't change them . . . Now it's your turn."

Craig considered it awhile. Then looked at her, smiling, let her know he was having fun. "How about . . ." He thought now, staring up at the ceiling. "You're jealous? You got left out of that world . . . maybe you would rather have been a boy. The academic life bores you. You don't know what to do with your life, but you see a chance to get back at Frank through me."

Colleen laughed. "You'll get the hang of it," she said.

The man at the next table was paying his check with a credit card, the teenager still aloof.

"Maybe she's his wife," Craig said as the pair walked out of the restaurant.

"Come on."

"His first wife died, he's got some money," Craig said, "and found a runaway teenager to marry him, fulfilling his fantasy. She seemed a little bored, though."

"That's ridiculous."

"The ridiculous is what you find here in sunny South Florida," Craig said. "It's the norm. And if you hang around long enough, you'll learn to always question your first impressions."

A waiter filled their glasses again, finishing the bottle. The combo was playing "Stompin' at the Savoy." Craig ran a finger around the rim of his wineglass.

"What are you thinking?" Colleen asked.

"I'm trying to remember if I snore or not." .

After all these years Frank Bishop was beginning to feel like an old fool, a cartoon character, the sucker, the hick being taken for a ride, awarded one minute to be robbed the next. Thinking that, he wondered if it had been set up all along, all in the same day.

First Johnny had called.

"Frank, your friend Gallanti is up to his neck in something. Don't ask me what because I can't tell you. What I can tell you is how it went down."

"That's a start, isn't it," Frank had said. "But first I'd like you to tell me something else."

"What's that, Frank?"

"That the other thing you were supposed to be doing for me down there is taken care of."

"Frank, it's ancient history. So old I've forgotten about it."

Frank wasn't sure. If it was ancient history, why hadn't he heard from Colleen? She should have been complaining. He didn't say anything, though.

"Now you ready for Gallanti?"

"Tell me."

"Gallanti went to a garage around here where he's having a bus serviced. That ring a bell?"

"I know about the bus."

"He was there for only a few minutes, actually on the bus, took a briefcase on, then came out and got into a cab that was waiting. I followed the cab to a hotel where Gallanti met a guy who's got his own case, more like a small suitcase. They were in a restaurant in the hotel, their cases on the table, both of them open, so they can look at what's inside. The place was deserted. You couldn't get near them without spooking them. Nobody went near them. They exchanged cases, and afterward Gallanti walked out and took a cab back to the bus. He left the case on the bus."

"That's it?"

"What more do you want?" Brown asked. "Is he up to something? Shall I stick with him?"

Frank thought about it. "You got nothing else to do, you might as well. But don't make a nuisance of yourself."

"I wouldn't dream of it," Brown said.

Little more than twelve hours later Frank got the second call. This one from Sly Gallanti himself.

"You won't believe it. We've been ripped off," Sly said.

He believed it. He didn't have to ask what Sly was talking about. All he wanted was to hear Sly tell him how it had happened. Just like Brown had described the action earlier. It was funny, as Sly talked he could hear also parts of Brown's conversation.

"Frank, I got mugged by a kid last night in the fucking park. I'd probably be dead if some guy hadn't come along and put a gun to the kid's head. The guy brought me back here to the Beach. Frank, I—"

He could picture Sly sitting in a hotel room, the air conditioner going in the middle of the winter in Florida. Maybe a couple of people around, maybe even a fuckin' script on the bed in front of him, everybody having a hard time not laughing. Frank felt like screaming. But he said quietly, "Just tell me what happened."

"Frank, it was like the whole thing was set up."

You bet it was, Frank thought. Right from the very

beginning. And he—Frank Bishop—was the all-time patsy. "What was set up?" Still calm.

"The guy drove straight to the garage where the bus is being repaired. He put the fuckin' gun on me and forced me to go over a goddamn fence, get the suitcase from the bus and give it to him. The case was full of product, Frank. I'd just put it on the bus earlier in the day—"

"Then what did he do? Drive you to your hotel?"

"As a matter of fact—"

"Come in and have a drink with you, a few laughs. You and John Brown?"

"Frank, I don't like what I'm hearing. . . . Are you suggesting I was in on this?"

"Were you, Sly?"

"Frank, I swear to God—"

"Don't say that," Frank said. "You'll bring more trouble on yourself than you've already got."

"Frank, I'm telling you what happened. You think I'm gonna call and tell you I'm cheating you?"

"Listen, I'm not going to try and understand your motives." He was having a hard time keeping control. "I just want that suitcase back on the bus. Or I want the money. One or the other. It's your choice, Sly. But do it. And do it fast."

"Who's John Brown?" Sly asked.

"The guy you set this up with." He hung up. Thinking maybe he'd have to go to Florida himself to straighten this mess out.

Craig got into bed while she was in the bathroom. When she came out she was wearing men's pajamas. Royal purple. She walked over, not looking at him, and fluffed the pillows on her bed, shy but not self-conscious. He watched her turn the covers back,

159

wondering what the hell he was doing here: whatever it was, he was beginning to enjoy it. "Are you all right?" she asked.

"Fine," he said. "I was wondering why you think it's so safe here. You think Brown can't find you?"

"He's got no reason to even look for me. But he's not very smart if he does."

"Why? Because of Frank? That didn't stop him from killing Carl."

"Which you claim was an accident. He intended to kill you." She got into bed. "Do you want to watch TV, or read?"

"I don't have anything to read," he said.

"I can give you my copy of *Huckleberry Finn.*"

"Thanks," Craig said, "but I'm fine, really. Playing house with you is fun. I like you. The thing is, I don't think Brown likes you. I'm not even so sure that he cares what Frank thinks. I wouldn't get too confident about Frank's influence over him."

"So what are you saying?"

"Tomorrow I'll find another place. And try to find Brown."

"Can we talk about it tomorrow?"

"We can talk about it, but I know what I'm going to do."

"But you don't know what Brown is doing. Will the light bother you if I read for a while?"

"No," he said. And closed his eyes. This all felt too damned domestic. Going to sleep, he saw himself taking the bathroom door off its hinges before he remembered where he was; with a girl young enough to be his daughter, whose father wanted him dead.

Seventeen

_J_ULIUS TOOK A SECOND CUP OF COFFEE DOWN TO THE porch. It was seven-thirty. He sat down across from Mrs. Duke. They played three games of checkers, Julius letting her win the last one. Then he sat back, lit a cigarette and pushed his straw hat forward, blocking out the sun that at this hour angled in over the tops of the palm trees along the beach and across his eyes. Colleen was late. She was usually here by this time when they would go out to breakfast. It worried him that Chappell was probably going to take up more of her time now.

John Leslie

A little before eight-thirty he saw Sly coming down the sidewalk toward the hotel. Walking fast like he was late for something. Twenty years in prison could slow a man down, but it hadn't had that effect on Gallanti.

"What's the hurry?" Julius asked. "You're moving like you had someplace to go."

"I talked to Frank," Sly said. He pulled a chair up next to Julius. "You were right. He thinks I'm stealing from him."

Julius nodded. "That's the way Frank Bishop's mind works. He sees the worst in every situation. He wasn't always like that, but he is now. What will you do?"

"You pull some weight with him, I thought you might talk to him for me."

"I'll call him, but it won't do any good. I've tried to talk to him about Colleen's problem and he won't even listen."

"What's her problem?"

"She's taken an interest in a guy Frank thinks killed his son, Carl. Frank's put out a contract on the guy. Colleen says he didn't do it. The guy says he didn't do it. Frank says he did, and guess who he's listening to."

Sly didn't say anything for a moment. "I guess then all I can do is find the son of a bitch who ripped me off."

"You know where to start looking?"

"Does the name John Brown mean anything to you?"

Julius looked at him in disbelief. "Jesus Christ," he said.

He looked up and saw Colleen standing on the porch.

"What's this about John Brown?" she asked.

* * *

162

Craig opened his eyes, thinking he'd get up quietly, dress and try to get out of the room without disturbing her. He looked at his watch. Jesus, the most he had slept since he went in the hospital. It was eight-thirty. He checked Colleen's bed. She wasn't in it. And the bathroom door was open. She had gotten up and out of the room without disturbing him. He got up, went into the bathroom, then dressed. He'd leave her a note, something humorous, upbeat, but letting her know that he appreciated all she'd done. He'd be in touch—something like that.

He was composing it on a sheet of hotel stationery when she walked in. She stared at him, a strange look in her eyes.

"Morning," he said. "What's the matter, you couldn't sleep?"

"You've seen John Brown, haven't you?" She was excited.

What was this all about? "Recently . . . no," he said.

"I mean, you've seen him. You know what he looks like."

"Yeah. I told you. I saw him standing in a window in Canada when he shot your brother."

"Could you describe him?"

"A few days ago I could have done better than that. I had a picture of him before the fire. Why? What's going on?"

"There's a man down at Julius's hotel who would like to talk to you. I told him I thought you'd be able to help him with Brown."

"You want to tell me what's going on?"

"Sly can tell you," she said.

Sylvester Gallanti. Another ancient guy. Colleen told him about Gallanti—Sly—as they walked along

163

Ocean Drive to the C-Breeze. Awed when she said that he'd once worked in Chicago for Al Capone. And that he'd been in prison the last twenty years. Craig was curious, as much about Gallanti himself as what he was going to say about John Brown.

But it was soon clear that Sly wasn't going to say anything about Brown, not in his presence. Shy Sly, you think he got this old talking to strangers who walked on the other side of the fence? Craig asked himself. And answered himself—no way. Sly was quiet, watchful. Not unfriendly, but he wasn't greeting Craig like a member of the Brotherhood either.

Julius said to Craig, "You're the only person here who's seen Brown. Sly would like to know what he looks like."

Looking at Sly, Craig wondered if he would have guessed the guy had done a lot of time. There was something about him, but it might not be prison, he thought. John Brown could spoil a guy's day too.

"I only saw him once, and not for long, standing in a window," Craig said. "I used to have a picture of him, but I can't tell you how long ago it was taken." He described Brown, a detailed cop's description, pausing once in a while to remember what he'd seen and what the photo showed. Brown's approximate weight, one eighty, one ninety, he thought; maybe six feet tall, with dark, curly hair, brown eyes, a swarthy complexion, bushy eyebrows, thick-lipped, with a prominent nose.

Sly listened, watching Craig, without any particular expression on his face.

"He looked Italian," Craig said. "If I had to, I could probably get another photo of him."

After a moment Sly turned to Julius. "I don't need a photo. That's him," Sly said.

There was silence. Julius said, "There you are. Now what are you going to do?"

Sly didn't say anything, looking at Craig.

Craig said, "If I knew what was going on I might be a little more help."

Colleen reached out to Sly. He gripped her small hand, holding it like he might lean over and kiss it. "He's all right," Colleen said.

"He's law," Sly replied.

"A couple times removed," Craig said. "We're maybe second cousins. A lot of the time we're not even on speaking terms."

"A bounty hunter," Julius said.

"Brown was a skip. My brother went up to Canada to bring him back and got killed for his effort. I went up, and lost him. I know Brown's back here, but the charges against him were dropped." He looked at Colleen. "I'm not after him—officially."

The three of them looked at Sly and waited.

"You know where he is?" Sly asked.

"I know somebody who does," Craig said.

"I want to see him," Sly said.

Craig said, "What for?"

"The son of a bitch ripped me off."

"And Frank Bishop," Julius added.

Craig glanced at Colleen again, who smiled back at him and shrugged.

"Frank? Does Frank know about it?"

"I told him a little while ago," Sly said.

"About Brown?"

"Frank mentioned Brown for some reason. Like Brown and I had planned the whole thing. That's why I wanted a description."

"Jesus," Craig said, "let me get this straight. You and Frank had a deal going that Brown interrupted.

Frank thinks you and Brown ripped him off. But according to you, Brown was working this on his own. Is that how you see it?"

"That's the way it looks."

"In the meantime Frank's got me on a hit list, and Brown's his hired gun."

"So I heard," Sly said.

"And you want me to take you to Brown."

"Just point me in the right direction. I'll be able to smell him," Sly said.

"Jesus Christ," Craig said. "Is there anybody who doesn't want a piece of this guy? I'll tell you what, you're next in line, but I've got the first shot at him. What's left will be yours."

Colleen gave him another smile. "How about if I hire you just to bring Brown in?" she said.

"Somebody's got to talk to Frank," Craig said. "Either you or Julius." He walked along the beach with her, on their way back to the Carlyle.

"What for?" Colleen asked.

"I've got a feeling Brown is fucking up. . . . Listen, I was leaving you a note this morning when you came in. I'm going to move into my office until I find a place to live."

"If that's what you want to do. But I am serious about hiring you to find Brown."

Craig smiled. "Why? You don't have to. I'm working for myself now."

"That's what I'm afraid of. You kill Brown and that makes you no different from him."

"You squeamish about how justice comes?"

"Yes," she said. "I don't want to see you in jail."

"You could bail me out and we could run to Canada."

"You can be pretty arrogant, you know that?"

"Uh-oh. Pretty soon you're going to start charging for these analytic sessions. I can't afford it."

"So don't do this on your own. Sly's going to need you too."

"When I find Brown I'll see what he says about it. I don't even know what he took, do you?"

"A hundred thousand dollars worth of coke."

"Jesus."

"Frank put up the money. Sly was going to run it back on the bus to New York and sell it."

"Okay, what I was getting at a minute ago—why you should call Frank is maybe Brown didn't know about that part, that Frank was involved. I can see Brown ripping off Gallanti, but not Frank. You see what I'm getting at?"

"Setting Brown and Frank against each other?"

"Exactly."

"There's more that Sly didn't tell you."

"What?"

"Brown followed him into a park in Miami and saved Sly's life from a mugger who attacked him."

"You're kidding."

"Then Brown offered to bring Sly back here, but stopped at the bus, forcing Sly to get the bag of coke he'd put on there the same day."

"So Brown had been following Sly all day, or else he knew where the stuff was going to be ahead of time."

"Does it make any sense?"

Craig thought for a minute. There were many possibilities. "Maybe," he said, "but I think it'll get clearer when you talk to Frank."

"What should I say?"

"Tell him the truth, what you just told me, and that Brown was the guy responsible. See what he says."

"Should I mention you?"

"I've been thinking about that. Frank thinks I'm

dead. You might want to do a little screaming at what Brown has done to me—let him go on thinking Brown has done his job."

"Anything else?"

"Yeah. What was Sly doing in Miami in a park at night?"

"Julius says he's gay. He was trying to pick up someone."

"Jesus, you run with quite a crowd."

They crossed the beach and went into the hotel.

What he had was a suitcase full of toot. His daddy would have known what to do with it, Brown thought. But he hadn't seen his daddy in twenty years, not since he and his mother left Flamingo Key and the big, bearded man who ruled the swamp in a thirty-five-foot fishing boat that he'd take out for two, three weeks at a time, coming back home with a sack full of money and his own personal supply of drugs.

His daddy would know what to do with it, but Brown didn't. He'd never dealt with drugs.

Brown had come to Miami as a kid, with his mother, when she left the old man in the swamp. Brown started working construction summers when he was fifteen. At sixteen he quit school and went to work full time but from a different angle: stealing tools and material from construction sites and hauling it to another county, where he fenced the stuff himself. Until he got caught one night by a couple of hired toughs paid to lay in wait for him. Instead of calling the cops, they worked him over. It took him three months to recover, and when he did he went north and got into organized labor, where the pay was more secure and he gave out the beatings. It was there he met Frank Bishop.

Drugs he didn't know shit about. Now he knew he

should have moved in on the old man before he went into the hotel, when he was carrying the briefcase.

He had put the suitcase inside a large, old steamer trunk that had belonged to Jeannie's grandmother and now sat at the foot of the bed in Jeannie's apartment. Let it stay there until he could figure out some way of getting rid of it. The thing was, he was beginning to worry now that if Frank found out that he had ripped off the old man, there was going to be trouble. He didn't know if Frank knew about the stash or not, although Frank hadn't seemed too concerned when he had talked to him earlier.

The faster he could get rid of that suitcase, though, the better he was going to feel. He would make some calls, see if he couldn't find somebody to take the stuff off his hands. The trouble was, he didn't have any idea of the value. What was he going to do, put it on the market, an ad in the paper, say, hey, make me an offer? There had to be another way.

Which was when he decided to sit on the stuff. Don't get uptight, just hang loose, let Frank call him. Maybe the Irishman would know the bag's value.

"Haven't I taken care of you?" Frank Bishop said. "All these years I've provided for you, given you work. I took you off the street when you were nothing but a two-bit hood on the take with some teamsters union in New Jersey. I brought you up through the ranks. You stumbled and fell, I was there to pick you up. I set you up with the feds even, gave you some legitimacy. And then when you get in deep, I give you cover, find accommodations for you in Canada. Put my son's life on the line to protect you. My only son."

John Brown listened, knowing where this was going. Like he was a kid who had to be reminded that someone else was responsible for every step he'd taken in life. It pissed Brown off, just listening to this shit, and he felt like banging the receiver down in Frank's ear. But he wouldn't do that; he couldn't afford to do that now.

"Frank, what is this all about?"

"What it's about," Frank said, "is trust. I asked you to do a simple job for me, but you saw an opportunity to go on your own. Did you think because I asked you to watch Sly that I didn't know what was going on? Or maybe that I'd never figure out that it was you who robbed me? I want the suitcase back, Johnny. Or a hundred grand. One or the other."

Brown couldn't believe it. Two days since he'd taken the fucking suitcase from Gallanti, and Frank was onto him.

Gallanti didn't know him from Adam, had probably never even heard of Brown. It was dark the night he'd saved Gallanti from the kid in the park, and the old man wasn't in any condition to remember much about anyone after nearly being choked to death, his face scratched and bleeding from having his head slammed into the bushes.

Brown wasn't going to admit to anything. He would have to bluff his way through it. "Frank, where do you get this stuff? Who's been talking to you?"

"Sly described you perfectly. It was a dumb thing to do."

"I don't believe it," Brown said.

"Twenty-four hours, Johnny. The product or the money. I want that bag returned to Sly at his hotel. You understand?"

What he understood was that he got his question answered without even asking it. It was worth a hundred grand. Even worth some trouble with Frank Bishop.

Eighteen

CRAIG DIDN'T LIKE IT; BROWN WAS JUST TOO UNPRE-dictable. Anything could happen. From their room in the Carlyle he'd listened to the one-sided conversation between Colleen and her father. After she'd hung up she told him that Frank was giving Brown just twenty-four hours to return the suitcase to Gallanti.

"Or else," Craig said.

Colleen shrugged. "I guess with Frank that's understood."

"But Brown isn't so predictable. I think he's probably over being threatened by Frank."

"Then you don't think he'll show up."

"Who knows what he'll do next." In that respect, Craig thought, he and Brown were alike: who knows even what I'm going to do.

Colleen sat in a chair by the phone, looking out the window of the oceanfront room. "Frank thinks you're dead," she said.

"He said that?"

"He said, 'Johnny's just been through this, only from the opposite end. He knows how it works.'"

"So Brown thinks he did his job."

She turned from the window. And smiling, said, "You're in the clear. As long as they don't know you're alive, we won't have to worry about you any longer."

He grinned back at her. "No, but now you've got somebody else to worry about."

"Who's that?"

"Sly Gallanti." Knowing now that he was in this, but beginning to see a way out.

They went back to the C-Breeze and told Julius and Sly. Sly said, "He's going to bring it back, huh?"

"Believe it when you see it," Craig said.

"Yeah, that's what I thought. But Frank knows what happened. He doesn't still think I was in on this?"

"It's hard to know what he thinks," Colleen said. "Apparently Brown was following you on Frank's orders the day you made your deal. Frank wanted to keep an eye on you . . . but Brown saw an opportunity, probably without even knowing Frank's involvement. Brown moved in. Frank isn't going to accept any of the blame—because he doesn't accept blame. It will make things easier if you get that suitcase back."

"Brown isn't going to bring it back," Julius said.

"Maybe with a little help." They turned toward

Craig. "We might be able to put a little more pressure on him," he said. Watching himself now beginning to set the thing up.

"You put more pressure on him than Frank does, the guy will explode," Julius said.

"Does anybody care?" Craig glanced around. No one said anything. An old lady dozed in a chair behind Colleen, a checkerboard beside her, her hands clasped in her lap. Except for the occasional rustle of her breath, she appeared dead. "Brown thinks I was killed in the fire," Craig said.

"He told Frank that," Colleen said.

"If he finds out he didn't do his job, that I'm still alive, maybe we have a better chance of drawing him out."

Julius lit a cigarette. "You know where he is. Why don't you just go get him?"

Craig looked at Colleen. "And maybe lose Sly's investment?" He grinned at Sly. "We're going to bring Brown to us."

"How?" Colleen asked.

"Sly's going to offer him a trade. Me for his suitcase. Is that a bargain?" He realized he was taking charge, and he felt better. It was almost as if he could see how it would end, had to end, and that it was inevitable, had been inevitable since Brown opened that door in Montreal and found Barry standing there holding a pair of handcuffs.

Sly said, "The tethered goat. Shall we slit your throat too? Give him the scent of blood."

Julius said, "You may only be a cousin, as you say, but you're still a lawman. You know what you're getting mixed up in?"

Craig smiled. Sure, it would be Julius who would have thought of it. He said, straight-faced now, "I'm bringing John Brown to justice—none of you seem to be bothered by that." It was like a falling out among thieves.

"I don't get it," Julius said. "What makes you think Brown will give up a hundred grand for you?"

Craig said, "He won't. He wants it all—me and the money. But when Sly threatens to tell Frank I'm still alive, Brown isn't going to have any choice."

"Jesus, you think the guy is dumb, he'll fall for that?" Sly asked.

"I don't know if he's dumb or not, but I think he wants to be rid of me as much as I do him."

It wasn't in his nature to worry, John Brown thought. What was the point? It was easier to do something than sit back thinking about it, and if you fucked up, then you either got a second chance or you didn't. In his lifetime he'd had little need of second chances. And the reason for that, he thought, was because he didn't get too excited over other people's priorities. He took things at his own pace, always waiting for the right moment to act, a sort of gut level instinct that had been honed over the years and that he'd come to rely on for its accuracy. Which was why he could put a gun to his head, like he had in Montreal, pull the trigger and know, *know,* that he would live.

But when the instinct failed him, Jesus, it didn't mess around. Like the business with the old man. He had fucked up. Now there had to be some way to turn it around, Brown was thinking, without having to pay too much for his mistake.

The main thing was not to be pressured by Frank. Take it easy, be methodical, sure-footed as one of the big cats back in the swamp, and he could still pull this off. Frank was getting old, losing his grip; he'd noticed a change in him since Carl was killed. Frank was on the warpath, pushing too hard, but at his age it was taking its toll fast. The possibility that Frank didn't have much time left was something to think about.

Frank had an empire he'd built. What the hell was going to happen to it? There was a daughter, but Brown never heard much about her. Come to think of it, though, hadn't Frank told him that she was in Florida? Yeah. She'd come down on the bus with the old man, Gallanti.

Now there was something to ponder. Maybe he'd been aiming too low all along; it was time to raise his sights. What was a hundred grand when there was a mountain of money sitting right in front of him?

The phone rang while he was pondering, and Jeannie said it was for him. A Sylvester Gallanti.

Shit. Now what? Why would Frank give Gallanti this number?

"Yeah," Brown said. Irritable, yet curious.

"Frank says you'll be coming by within the next few hours."

"Coming by where, what for and to see who?"

"My hotel to return the stuff you stole from me the other night."

"Fuck you."

"John, that's a bad attitude. You steal from a man and get caught, the man's nice enough to let you return the stuff, no questions, you ought to be grateful. Bring it back with a smile on your face."

"You think I've got something of yours," Brown said, "come and get it." He'd mess with the old guy awhile, see how far he was willing to go with this. "Or I'll tell you what, send one of your little sweethearts from the park over here, let him get it for you."

"How 'bout if I send Craig Chappell?"

175

"Who?"

"What's the matter, John, you suddenly lose your hearing? I said, Craig Chappell."

What was this shit now? He was being played with. Another old man was messing with him. What would Frank know about Chappell who was supposed to be dead.

"John, you run out of smart-ass things to say?"

"Fuck you." Aware though that his voice wasn't the same now.

"All right. Here's how it goes. You bring the bag to the hotel and you leave it at the desk with the clerk. Give him my name. They'll hold it for me. Once I get that suitcase I'll give you Chappell. But if I don't get it today, Johnny, Frank's going to know just how badly you fucked up."

Brown thought quickly. Whatever he did, he wasn't going to be pushed into anything, let somebody else set the rules. "I ain't walking into any hotel with it," he said.

There was a pause, no sound from the phone, like somebody's hand had been placed over the mouthpiece. Gallanti came back on. "What's your pleasure, then?" Sarcastic.

Brown smiled, his confidence back. "Midnight on the beach at Tenth Street and Ocean Drive. I want Frank's daughter, what's her name—Colleen—to make the pickup. I want to be able to see Chappell down by the water . . ." He paused.

"That's all you want?" Still the sarcasm in his voice.

"For now," Brown said. "If I think of anything else I'll let you know."

"Yeah, well I'm not going with that scene."

Brown said, "You don't have any choice. Not if you want your product."

"I'll get back to you."

"Fuck you," Brown said. But Gallanti had hung up on him. Just like that. Put the phone down in his ear.

Brown replaced the receiver and turned, pissed off. Jeannie was standing behind him. "What was that all about?" she asked.

"It was about nothing," he said. "I want you to be ready to go to Delray tonight, stay with your mother awhile. I want you to give something to somebody, and then I want you to drive up there. You better call her, make arrangements."

"Why?"

"Stop asking me questions," he shouted. "Just do what I tell you." Brown crossed the room, going to the bedroom, where he could think, when he suddenly stopped and turned back to Jeannie. "I'm gonna need a car. Call around the agencies, see if you can find me a Jeep wagon, something with smoked windows." The thing was coming together now. Unless Gallanti fucked it up.

"Well," Sly said.

"Not bad," Craig said. "You could get a cameo role playing an old gangster in the movies."

"They already made that picture. Kirk Douglas and Burt Lancaster. They were pretty good."

"What happens now?" Colleen asked.

"Call him back," Craig said. "Brown isn't calling the shots and Colleen isn't a part of this. How did he know about her anyway?"

"Frank probably told him," she said. "But I'll do it."

"No. I've made two mistakes already with Brown. I'm not going for a third."

"But it isn't me he wants."

Craig thought a moment. "Call him back," he said

John Leslie

to Sly. "Tell him to bring the stuff back where he got it. To the bus at midnight. No other deal. Otherwise I go to Frank, threaten to have Brown charged with attempted murder. Put the Metro Dade police after him. Frank isn't going to let Brown get near a courtroom any more now than he was when he sent him to Montreal."

"And if Brown says no?"

"I've got a better idea. I'll talk to him. He won't say no."

He found a Jeep Cherokee that was perfect, with dark tinted windows. Jeannie was on her way to Delray Beach, and he'd picked up the steamer trunk from her apartment with the suitcase in the bottom of it. He put the trunk in the back of the Jeep.

The fucking bounty hunter was in for a surprise. The guy wanted to play cowboy. That threatening tone, giving Brown instructions like he was some kind of frightened kid—like he was afraid of Frank Bishop. Fuck Frank. Frank was going to get a surprise too.

The bounty hunter had said, "You bring the case back where you got it. At midnight."

Brown said, "Yeah, and then what happens?"

"Then it's you and me, just the two of us." What were they going to do, shoot it out on the street?

Shit. Brown knew better than that. He said, "I'll think about it," and hung up. There. Hung up on the bounty hunter. But he did think about it, and figured out what he had to do; he'd take the case back, all right, but that was the only thing that would fit into the bounty hunter's plan.

Brown looked at his watch. A little more than ten hours until midnight. The witching hour. A lot could happen in ten hours.

178

Nineteen

I'M COMING WITH YOU," COLLEEN SAID. THEY WERE walking down Collins Avenue, Colleen taking two steps to one of Craig Chappell's. She felt like a kid again. "Julius and Sly are going to be on the bus. I want to be there."

"No," Craig said. "There's no reason for you to be there."

"What reason is there for Julius or Sly to be there?"

"I may need them."

"Two old men? Come on! What can they do?"

"Provide years of experience in this kind of thing."

"You're being macho again."

Craig didn't say anything. She walked, aware of the traffic on Collins without really seeing or paying attention to it. It was just noise. She knew why she was being so insistent: she wanted to see John Brown, the man who had killed her brother. She wanted to see how Craig handled him: she was certain that Craig was planning to kill him. That bothered her, but something else bothered her even more . . .

"Have you got a plan?" she asked.

"What are you talking about?"

"Do you know how you're going to do it?"

"Do what?"

"Kill Brown."

"Listen," Craig said, "I didn't say I was going to kill him."

"But you are. You want to. That's all you think about, getting back at him for what he did to your brother."

"I don't know what's going to happen."

She laughed. "You know you aren't going to take him in. Not on a drug charge. Watch him spend five years in jail, maybe not even that." She paused. "What are you going to do about the drugs?"

Craig slowed his pace and looked at her. "What do you think I'm going to do about them?"

"I don't think they're going to Sly," she said.

He looked up the street, picking up the pace again.

"You kill Brown and turn over the drugs to the cops, he will be just another dead drug dealer, Craig Chappell bringing him to justice, taming the wild frontier. Isn't that the way you see it?"

"You've got a good imagination."

"Stop cowboying," she said.

"And do what? What do you want me to do?"

"Just remember you're not a cop."

"I used to be," he said.

"This is Sly's life," she said. "It's all that he's got left. I don't like it, but I don't want to see him become another one of Frank's victims. Give him a chance."

"Chances don't mean anything to a dead man," Craig said.

She was about to tell him he sounded like a pompous ass but changed her mind. They walked over to Ocean Drive in silence and moments later went up the porch of the C-Breeze, where Julius was dozing in his chair.

The cowboy was alive all right, but he wasn't in one piece. Brown was sitting in the Jeep when they came out of the hotel where he had tailed Gallanti a few days ago. The cowboy and the lady, the cowboy with his arm in a blue sling. The lady, a perky little thing, looked like she was about eighteen, her short legs pumping away as she tried to keep up with the cowboy. Brown stayed a block behind them in the Jeep, pulling over to the curb to keep that distance. When they turned off Collins he drove to the corner and watched as they walked to Ocean Drive and turned right. Driving to that intersection, he saw them go into another hotel, the C-Breeze. Brown parked at a meter and waited.

Hell, it'd be easy to park right in front of the hotel and wait for them to come out, gun the son of a bitch down as they stepped onto the sidewalk. But he was curious now about the lady, and he wanted to be able to look the cowboy in the eyes this time, let the guy see his killer.

But that could wait. Cowboy wasn't going anywhere. It was the lady Brown was concentrating on now, because there was a lady somewhere in the picture he was looking for. Frank Bishop's daughter

181

was in Miami. He wouldn't expect her to be hanging out with the cowboy, but it didn't hurt to know all the players in the game when you were playing for high stakes. He had underestimated the cowboy before; he wouldn't do it again. Brown looked at his watch. Ten past five.

Ten minutes later the cowboy and the lady and another old man came out of the hotel and walked right past the Jeep parked at the curb without even looking at it. Brown watched in the rearview mirror as they got to the intersection and the cowboy and the old man turned up the street. The lady continued on Ocean Drive. Brown made a U-turn and dropped in behind her.

They went into the Strand, Julius telling Craig how Meyer Lansky had Bugsy Siegel bumped off. They went to the bar and ordered a drink, waiting for Colleen to join them once she got back from the Carlyle, where she'd gone to freshen up. The thing was, Julius explained, to get the guy with somebody he trusted, where he could relax. Then you hit him. This thing with Brown was too out in the open, he knew what was coming. The guy would never show up.

Craig listened, patient, fascinated by the old man's stories—the good old days, and the old ways were the best—realizing that Julius lived in a different time frame. He could only absorb so much before it got tangled up with the past. His mind was still sharp, but every new experience was compared, related to something similar he had been through in the past. If not, he wouldn't think about it at all. Julius wasn't street-tough the way Sly was, but he loved being in the midst of the action, more as an officer, a sort of honorary chief executive, than a soldier.

Craig said to Julius, "I don't want Colleen in on this."

Julius sipped his gin. "Tell her, then."

"I told her. She won't listen to me."

"That doesn't surprise me." Julius speared a large, green olive from the bottom of his glass and ate it. "What makes you think she'll listen to me?"

"You seem to have a stronger influence on her," Craig said.

Julius looked thoughtful. "Yeah, I suppose I do. But one reason maybe is because I've never tried to tell her what to do. I listen to her but I don't interfere."

"She respects you . . . but I think you ought to get her to open up a little more. She's got her problems too."

He looked at Craig, frowning slightly. "What are you talking about?"

"See? You don't know." Craig wasn't surprised. "She talks to you, confides in you, but she doesn't tell you everything. Somebody should have been listening to this kid a long time ago."

"What is this? If Colleen's got a problem, I want to know about it."

Craig stared at him, saw the thin web of blue veins around his temples. Why hadn't she told him? "Colleen tried to take her life not long ago."

Julius put his glass down, his hand trembling. Craig watched him lean against the bar, thinking he probably shouldn't have told him; a guy this old, he looked strong, all the stuff he'd seen over the years, but Jesus . . . maybe he had a weak heart.

Julius took another sip of gin. "She didn't tell me."

"Probably didn't want to upset you."

Julius shook his head. "A girl her age, all she's got going for her. Why would she do something like that?"

183

"She had problems over the years with Frank, things she'd never worked out. And she was under a lot of pressure at school. It got to her."

Julius said, "Why'd she tell you?"

"I've thought about that," Craig said. "The first time I met her I was looking for Brown. I told her some things about my life that she seemed to respond to. Maybe it made a difference, I don't know. But later she confided in me. The other thing, and I believe this . . . she got it out of her system. I don't think you have to worry about Colleen any more. She's able to deal with it, even though she might not talk to you about it, or anyone in the family."

"What happened with Frank?"

"Listen," Craig said, "she probably didn't want you to know this, or she would have told you."

"I want to know about Frank."

"He messed around with her when she was a kid," Craig said.

"Jesus Christ."

"You didn't know?"

"I'll tell you, I always wondered about that with Frank. I tried a couple times to talk to Colleen then, but she said there was nothing wrong."

"She was bottling it up."

Julius rapped the bar with his clenched fist. "The son of a bitch," he said. "Frank never should have been a father. I should have known."

"What?"

Julius shook his head. "I just should have known."

Craig nodded, something coming to him, remembering when he first talked to Colleen on the phone that time when he was Craig Simmons with Connections, trying to dig up her past. She'd said, "Did Julius talk to you?"

He decided to take a chance. "You know who her parents were, don't you? Her real parents."

Julius looked at him and swallowed more gin. But he nodded, his eyes watery. Craig didn't think it was from the gin.

"Who's her father?" Craig asked.

Julius turned away, folded his arms, the fingernails of one hand digging into the slack flesh of his arm. "I am," he said.

Brown followed her to the Carlyle, parked quickly in front of the hotel and watched through the glass door as she picked up her key and got into the elevator. Then he walked in, went up to the desk and said to the desk clerk, "The woman who just came in, I've got an urgent message for her."

Surprised when the clerk said: "Miss Bishop, Room 211."

Jesus, he couldn't believe it. Colleen Bishop, right here, up two floors from him, all alone. What she had been doing with the cowboy, he couldn't figure out, but that wasn't important. She was here and she was alone. That was important. He didn't want to spook her now by calling her, or going up to the room, giving her a chance to alert the cowboy. He'd give her some time, see if she came out. If not, then he could work on another plan.

He went into the bar, sat at a table where he could watch the lobby, and ordered a beer, which he paid for. It was five-thirty. At five after six she came off the elevator, in different clothes now and scrubbed pretty. He finished his beer and followed her out the door.

She turned up the street, walking back in the direction she'd come. Brown jumped in the Jeep and followed her to the next block, where she turned up a side street that had no traffic, walking toward Collins Avenue. He stepped on the gas and raced to the middle of the block, turning up an alley that served as an access for the garbage trucks that picked up for the hotels fronting Ocean Drive.

This had to be as good a place as any.

Brown squealed to a halt and got out of the Jeep just as Colleen approached the alley. He stepped out from behind the Jeep and walked toward her. She glanced around nervously and then looked straight ahead.

Brown grabbed her by the arm and said, "Hey, baby."

She started to scream, but he pulled her into his body, her head forced just below his chest, choking off the sound. And stood there hugging her like they were in a loving embrace, except she was kicking and flailing her arms. "Stop it," he said, "or I'll fucking squeeze the life out of you right here."

He carried her in one arm to the Jeep and shoved her into the back like a rag doll next to Jeannie's steamer trunk. And climbed in behind her, hidden now behind the smoked glass. He picked the .45 from under the seat. She stared at it and calmed down.

"What do you want with me?"

"For now I want you in the trunk. We'll work out some more fun things later." He opened the trunk and took out the aluminum suitcase. "You can get in, or I'll stuff you in. Take your pick, Colleen."

She looked inside the trunk, seemed to think about it and then got in. "John Brown," she said, squatting inside the trunk.

He grinned at her. "Colleen Bishop," he said. "Now we know each other." He tied her hands and feet with rope from the trunk.

"Do you think Frank's going to let you get away with this?"

"Fuck Frank," Brown said. He stuffed a rag in her mouth and closed the lid on the trunk.

"I was forty-eight, maybe forty-nine, the last thing I was thinking about was babies," Julius said. "But I had to start thinking about it when my wife . . . God, it seems like yesterday. She was forty-four I think when she got pregnant. And she wanted the baby."

Craig nodded, listening, understanding.

"We'd been married fifteen years. She'd wanted a kid, but in all that time nothing happened. And then bang! Out of the blue, at that age, when we both thought it was all over. What am I going to do, tell her to forget it, get an abortion? She was determined. So I thought, what the hell, I can take an early retirement, help raise the kid, and I'll only be coming up on seventy when she's grown and out of the house."

The old man's eyes were tearing. "You know what's coming, don't you," Julius said.

Craig nodded. "I've got an idea."

"We had a beautiful daughter, but my wife died giving birth."

"Jesus," Craig said. Julius was on his second gin. He waited as the old man took a drink.

"There was Frank. I'd known the guy for a long time," Julius said. "He was seven, eight years younger than me. They wanted a kid, and I thought at least I'd be able to see her, which I wouldn't if I gave her up to an agency."

"Then Carl was born a couple years later."

"A year later, I think."

"And Frank lost interest in Colleen."

"Yeah, now he had a son. And when Frank's wife died when Colleen was twelve, I guess things got even worse."

"You never discussed any of this with Frank?"

187

John Leslie

Julius scoffed. "You never met Frank—he doesn't discuss anything."

Craig didn't say anything for a moment, just sat there nursing his drink, waiting. Then he said, "I won't mention this to Colleen, tell her I talked to you."

Julius nodded. "What's taking her so long anyway?"

Craig looked at his watch. It was 6:35. She'd been gone over an hour. "Christ, she was just going to shower and change clothes. I'd better get over there. If she comes in, keep her here."

The phone rang in Sly Gallanti's room. Sly picked it up.

"There's a messenger on his way over with a key to a baggage locker down at the bus station," Brown said. "You can pick up your suitcase there."

"You were supposed to bring it here," Sly said.

"Things aren't working the way they're supposed to." Brown laughed.

Sly was about to say something but heard the distant hum of a dead line as Brown hung up.

_____ *Twenty*

*T*HE SUITCASE WAS ON THE BED, ITS TOP OPEN. SLY SAT ON
the edge of the bed, his hand resting on the lip of the
empty case. Julius sat slumped in a chair facing the
bed. Craig stood in front of the window and read the
note they'd found inside the case. He read it aloud for
maybe the fifth time, but more like he was reading it to
himself than to the others, slowly, pausing after
certain words, his mind wandering as he tried to make
the events of the past few hours all fit together. The
message read:

To the cowboy bounty hunter:

   You aren't calling the shots anymore. If you want to see the girl alive, get in touch with Frank Bishop. He will tell you what to do. Don't try anything else. If you do, the girl will die. Slowly and painfully.

He had talked to the receptionist at the desk. A man fitting Brown's description had delivered the suitcase, asking them to keep it for Mr. Gallanti. No one noticed if Brown had arrived in a car, a cab, or on foot. Craig had gone to the Carlyle and found the same thing. A man, apparently Brown again, had asked for Colleen Bishop's room number. The receptionist remembered Colleen going out and leaving her key. She hadn't seen Brown again.

Which seemed to indicate that Brown had moved in on Colleen when she left the Carlyle on her way to meet them at the Strand. Somebody must have seen them; there must have been a struggle. She wouldn't have gotten into his car voluntarily. Unless he was holding a gun on her. He looked at Julius slumped in the chair. The father she didn't know.

Craig turned to Sly. "What kind of car was he driving the night he brought you back here?"

"I don't know one car from another. It was red, a sports car, I guess."

Craig thought he could probably have the car traced, either in Brown's name or Jeannie's, but he doubted it would do any good. Just like he could go around to the apartment on Biscayne, sure that he'd find no one home. He could check the car rental agencies, but that was going to take time.

He called Jeannie's apartment, no answer. He called the Omni where she had worked in the lounge and someone there told him she was on vacation.

That left Frank Bishop.

"Julius, you ought to call Frank. See if he's heard from Brown."

Julius looked up, tired, the strain showing in his face. "What if he hasn't?"

"Tell him to expect a call, that Brown has kidnapped Colleen."

Brown drove west on the Tamiami Trail, route 41, that crossed the state between Miami and Naples, cutting through the Everglades. Once they were out of Miami he pulled off the road and crawled into the back to check on Colleen. He opened the trunk and her large, dark eyes stared up at him in fear.

"How we doin', sweet thing?" Brown said. "You got enough air in here? We don't want you dyin' on us—not yet anyway." Brown grinned.

He checked the ropes binding her feet and hands and took the gag from her mouth. She gulped air. "You be good now," he said, "and I'll leave this thing open so you got plenty of air. We've got some traveling to do."

"Where are you taking me?"

Brown chuckled. The little lady was coming to life. She looked like she had some spark in her. "I'll bet you never been in a swamp before," he said. "Seen all those creepy, crawly things."

"What do you want?"

She reminded him of Jeannie, always asking questions. He wondered if she'd remind him of Jeannie in other ways. That would give him something to think about driving down this boring stretch of road. "You'll find out soon enough," he said. "For now, just make yourself comfortable. It can't be too bad in there, layin' on a hundred thousand dollars. Look at you. You didn't know that was the bottom of your bed, a hundred grand in white powder."

She said, "Why—" and he shoved the rag back in her mouth.

"Later," Brown said, and crawled back behind the wheel.

A couple hours later he turned off 41 onto an alternate asphalt road that led back into the swamp. Just in case the cowboy had been able to link him with the rented Jeep. Even though it was in Jeannie's name, if Chappell was as smart as he thought he was, he would have checked that too. But knowing Brown had rented a Jeep and finding him were two different things. Brown was sure the cowboy wasn't going to the cops. But just to be on the safe side Brown decided to take this little-used road that wound around through the swamp and would bring him back out on 41 twenty or twenty-five miles farther up the road.

Besides, he liked it back in here, felt comfortable, at home. The narrow road was bordered by a dense thicket of mangroves, swamp trees, and bushes, and in the gathering darkness he could see the shadows the Jeep headlights created in the dim light which was choked out by the heavy growth. It was beautiful in here, and terrifying. No cars, only one or two houses spread out.

He wondered what would have happened to him if his mother hadn't left his daddy and the swamp and brought him to Miami when she did. He'd have lived his life in here, probably have made his living wrestling alligators for tourists.

Which was better? Having a 'gator snapping at you, or Frank Bishop? It didn't matter, he decided. He could handle 'em both.

Dear-God Frank. The holier-than-thou fuck. He'd

been doing Frank's dirty work for too many years now. It was time Frank learned—or at least recognized the value of someone who had served too long as a foot soldier.

Frank was going to recognize his value soon enough.

Brown punched the accelerator and the Jeep skipped and banged across the potholed asphalt.

Twenty minutes later, coming back to the intersection with the Tamiami Trail, he pulled up by a dilapidated frame house that was a gas station, convenience store, and café which looked like it had been there for a hundred years, with its old gas pumps and rusty signs advertising Coke and chewing tobacco. It was now dark, the place closed for the night. Brown stopped beside the building, where two modern Southern Bell phone boxes were mounted, and got out. He called Frank Bishop collect.

When Frank accepted the call, Brown said, "You got twenty-four hours to get $500,000 together if you want to see Colleen again. Stay close to the phone." And hung up.

Julius said, "Frank, we don't know how it happened. She was coming to meet us—"

"Us who?" Frank demanded.

Julius hesitated, looked up at Craig standing in the hotel room, listening while Sly paced the floor. "Chappell," he said.

Frank said, "Julie, I don't believe it. What are you doing to me? First my son, now Colleen, and you tell me you're sitting in a bar having drinks with the guy who killed Carl . . . waiting for Colleen."

Julius raised his voice. "He didn't kill Carl. . . . Colleen's been trying to tell you that, but you won't listen. John Brown killed him, and it was Brown who stole that bag from Sly. It's sitting here now right in

193

front of me. Empty. Just the way Brown returned it. It's time you woke up, Frank. Chappell isn't your problem."

Frank didn't say anything.

Julius said, "John Brown saw a way to get to you, Frank. He's going to take you to the cleaners, and without Chappell there's not a damn thing you can do about it. Not if you want to see Colleen again."

"What's Chappell got to do with it?"

"It looks like Brown is setting him up. There was a note in the suitcase. He wants Chappell to be the courier."

"With half a million dollars of my money? Johnny's crazy . . . I've made mistakes but I'm not stupid," Frank said.

"What choice do you have? You going to call in the police—maybe your friends at the federal level, since you're dealing with a kidnapping? They'd love to come in, take Brown . . . then come after you. Come on, Frank."

There was another silence.

Julius sat up in his chair. "What did he say, how does he want you to handle it?"

"He wants the money together in twenty-four hours. He's calling back with instructions." Frank sounded like he'd lost some of his thunder.

Julius said, "Do it, Frank. We don't have any choice in this. Once we get Colleen out we can take care of Brown."

"I can take care of him now. I've got five guys I can have down there in the time it takes to get them on a plane."

"Frank, you may be dealing with a psycho. You don't know what Brown's going to do next. He's got Colleen. We've got to get her out. We're clear on that, aren't we, Frank?"

"I've got to think," Frank said.

"Think about Colleen."

Frank hung up. Julius replaced the receiver. Craig said, "What's he going to do?"

"I don't know," Julius replied.

Everglades City was much as he remembered it when he brought Jeannie here for a weekend once about five years ago. The fishing camp where they stayed was still there, on the outskirts of town, or what passed for a town, at the edge of the swamp along a wide channel weaving through the mangroves out into the Gulf. There were two vacant cabins available, and Brown took one that was isolated from the rest, set back from the water's edge among some Australian pine trees.

He backed the Cherokee along the side of the cabin. He walked to the front door, unlocked it and went in. One big room with a double bed, a couple of chairs, a small electric stove, a refrigerator, and a bathroom. A perfect place to hole up. No TV, but there was a telephone.

There was a back door that opened on to the secluded pines. Brown went out, walked to the Jeep and opened the rear door. Before driving in here he'd closed the trunk and locked it. He now pulled it from the back of the Jeep, eased it down to the ground and dragged it into the cabin via the back entrance. With the cabin doors closed and locked, he now opened it.

Colleen stared up at him. Hatred had replaced the fear that had been in her eyes earlier. Brown grinned down at her. "Kind of tight quarters," he said. "You want to stretch your legs, get some of the kinks out?" Wondering just how kinky she could get.

He reached down and took her by the hand. She winced and tried to pull away. Brown let her go. "All right," he said. "Do it your way. But try anything funny and you go back in there." He watched, grinning, as she eased herself up to a standing position. She was young. You could bend her like a pretzel, Brown thought, and she'd snap right back. He could see some bruises on her legs and arms. Her blond hair was disheveled, dark pouches under her eyes. It excited him.

"In Montreal," he said, watching her as she shook first one leg, then the other, rubbing her arms and wrists, "I read about this, a woman locked in a chest in a hotel room. I told your brother about it. Funny, I was shacked up with him for a couple a weeks, now I'm with you. I'll take you any day."

She didn't look at him, perhaps wouldn't look at him, which pissed him off. "The woman died in the goddamn chest," he said. "The hotel staff found her, got a whiff of her, after a week or so."

She remained standing in the center of the room, staring at the floor as she exercised her limbs. Brown slapped her face lightly and she looked up, angry, staring at him. Yeah, she was tough. Not like fat Carl. "You don't give a shit, do you?" he said. "So how about I put you back in there, test your air supply? What do you think, two hours, three?"

"What happened to Carl?" she demanded. Like she wasn't even listening to him. She rolled her head around, massaging her neck while still looking at him. He wanted to hit her again, a little harder this time.

"The fat slob stepped in front of a bullet," Brown said.

"But you shot him?" Her head remained still.

Brown grinned. "Yeah, I shot him. What difference does it make? It was an accident."

She turned away and started to walk around the

room, limping slowly, looking at the place. He pulled the gun from his waistband and walked beside her.

"Why are you doing this? What do you want with me?"

"I'd like to know what you're worth to Frank," Brown said.

She paused, like she was struck by some thought, then took a step and walked to the window. He stood behind her. She stared out the window for a while. Then turned, a strange expression on her face, not anger, but not smiling either. She said, "Yes, I'd like to know that too."

_____ *Twenty-one*

WHEN HE CAME IN, SOMETIME AFTER TWO A.M., FROM questioning hotel staff at the Carlyle and checking Jeannie's apartment, Craig found Sly and Julius dozing in chairs. Sly woke up, told Craig to take the bed.

"You get to be this age, you don't need to get in a bed to sleep," Sly said. "I knew a guy in prison never laid down all the time he was in there. He had asthma. He laid down, he couldn't breathe, or else he'd choke to death. Said he hadn't been to bed in five years before he was locked up. He slept just fine sitting up. He was a grandfather. At home he had a rocking chair he lived in. He killed his wife because she had Alzheimer's, didn't know what she was doing most of the time, and was in pain. He was sixty-five and he thought he probably wouldn't live more than a couple years. As far as I know he's still inside. He'd be close to eighty now. That'd make twenty years he never laid down."

Craig slept on top of the bed, in his clothes. He would wake up sometimes and hear the two old men talking in the dark. He would think about Colleen, see Brown's face in the window in Montreal and hear his voice on the tape recorder. And knew when he saw Brown again he would kill him. He went back to sleep and dreamed about Barry. Later he heard the door open and someone went out. When he woke up again he smelled coffee. It was morning; sunlight streamed into the room. Steam rose from Styrofoam cups of coffee on the table. Sly and Julius sat in the same chairs they'd slept in, sipping their coffee.

Craig got up and sat on the edge of the bed and looked at his watch. Seven o'clock. Julius handed him a cup. "Sly went out and got it," Julius said.

"It looks like a day of sitting and waiting," Sly said.

"You guys can get out of here from time to time, but I think it's better that Julius talks to Frank when he calls."

"If he calls," Julius said.

"He'll call," Craig said. "Brown will see to that."

"Yeah, and in the meantime, while we sit around waiting, what's going to happen to Colleen?"

"I'm going to get a check on the car rental agencies and look up a contact with the cops. There's nothing you can do now except wait."

"I'm going for a walk," Sly said. "I never was any good at waiting. You'd think after twenty years . . ." He stood up, shaking his head, and left the room.

Julius laced his fingers together, bending them back until the knuckles cracked.

She woke up thinking, thank God he didn't touch me. He'd tied her hands in front of her and then attached a short length of rope to his left ankle and the rope binding her hands. He'd pulled a chair over for her to sit on, or if he were in the right position, she might be able to stretch out on the floor. She didn't; she remained in the chair.

Sleep had come only after several hours of squirming and listening to Brown lying on top of the bed, snoring. She guessed maybe she'd slept for an hour or two, waking up when the first light came through the windows. Brown continued to snore. Each time he'd turned, he pulled against her weight.

After tying her up he lay on the bed grinning at her, the gun he carried placed under his pillow.

He'd said, "I'm tired. It's been a long day. We'll party tomorrow." Then turned the bedside light off and fell asleep almost at once.

Now she sat in the chair dreading the moment when he would wake up. Trying to think of ways to divert his attention, to keep his mind off whatever plans he might have for "partying" with her. If he touched her . . . she tried not to think about it.

And she had to pee. She tried not to think about that either, but the pressure was constant. If she woke him so she could get to the bathroom, it would give him ideas; he would probably want to stand there and watch. She thought about peeing on the floor, right here, now. Getting it over with. Then decided no, she would hold it as long as she could. It was so humiliating.

It was happening all over again, reduced to life's lowest common denominator, living like an animal in fear. She thought about getting her hands on the gun or even into the bathroom where she could lock the door and lay on the floor, alone, unbothered.

The memories were painful.

She looked at Brown with disgust. He was snoring evenly now, his left ankle stretched out toward her. All she had to do was lean forward and undo the several knots he had tied, then slip the end of the rope from beneath his leg, and she would be free.

She leaned forward, her hands outstretched, trembling slightly. She touched the first knot. Brown remained still, the rhythm of his breathing unchanged. She undid the knot slowly, holding her breath, careful not to touch him, not to touch the bed as she leaned over it.

She undid a series of three half-hitches and then sat back in the chair, breathing through her nose. The only sound now was Brown snoring, and some mockingbirds outside beginning the morning's love song.

All she had to do was pull away the rope that lay in the slight gap under his stockinged ankle. Then she could take half a dozen steps to the door and escape.

She waited until she was breathing evenly, then began slowly but steadily to pull the rope toward her, nine, maybe ten inches, and inch by inch it came to her. He snorted once and she stopped pulling, waiting until his breathing evened out again. Two inches to go and she was free.

When the rope finally slipped from under him, she felt exhausted but almost a feeling of relief. She sat back for a moment, pausing as she gathered the rope in her hands and looked at Brown, the rise and fall of his chest, then looked at the door.

She stood up, took a breath, turned her back on the bed and took one step toward the door. Brown said, "Morning, sweet thing. Going somewhere, are we?"

And she heard him thumb back the hammer of the gun.

She kept her back to him. "I have to go to the bathroom," she said.

"Hey, we all have to make pee-pee in the morning. It's natural; the first thing you do is get up and take a leak. But you don't have to be so secretive about it. All you had to do was ask me. Turn around, sweet thing; look at me when I'm talkin' to you."

She turned and looked into the barrel of the gun pointed at her.

"That's better. Now come over here. Sit down. Let's take those bracelets off your hands."

She walked back to the chair and let him untie the rope around her wrists. More frightened now because he sounded so syrupy. But she controlled it, concentrated on not showing any emotion, staring at him as he untied the ropes. "There, that's better, huh? Now you want to go pee-pee, go on."

She stood and started for the bathroom, got halfway across the room and heard the bed squeak as Brown got up. "Maybe I ought to go with you," he said, coming up behind her. "Make sure there's nothing in there going to frighten a sweet thing."

She was calm, didn't even have to go to the bathroom now. She said, "It's all right. I don't have to go that bad anyway."

Brown grinned at her, holding the gun in his hand. "Well, I do," he said. The syrup gone. "You can go in with me, watch me drain old Long John Hancock." He pushed her forward into the bathroom and closed the door behind them. "There now. You stand right there, you can even hold the big guy for me." He unzipped his pants.

She said, "I won't touch it."

Brown put the gun to her head and said, "You aren't with the grandpas and a cripple anymore, so don't tell me what you will and won't do."

"You make me touch that and you'll be a cripple."

He looked at her a moment, then grinned again. "Yeah," he said. "You got a point." She turned her head away as he took it out of his pants and began to pee. A steady hard stream that filled the room with an unusually strong stench of urine that made her want to gag. When he finished he said, "Your turn."

"I don't have to go," she replied.

He shrugged, flushed the toilet and led her back into the bedroom. And said, "Well, then, we better figure out something to do for the next few hours, since you got me up so early."

She said, "Tell me about Craig Chappell. . . . What did he do to you?"

"He didn't do nothin' to me. He's the one walkin' around with a broken arm and no place to live."

"Why are you trying to kill him?"

"Come on! You know why. If you don't, ask your daddy. . . . You want to lay on the bed for a while?"

"No," she said.

"I mean just to lay down. So I can keep my eye on you . . . don't have to tie you up again right now."

"You don't have to tie me up. I want to hear what happened in Montreal." She huddled on the chair, her arms folded, wrapping herself in a protective custody she didn't feel. From now on everything was going to be a front, just for show; she was scared.

Brown sat down on the edge of the bed. Grinned at her and said, "You want to hear about Montreal? All right. I'll tell you. Chappell sent his brother up to get me. He didn't tell you?"

She shook her head.

"Sent his kid brother up to do a man's job and I had to kill him."

She didn't say anything.

"You know how he found me?"

Again she didn't speak.

"They put a wiretap on my phone, my girlfriend's phone in Miami." Brown whistled. "Big brother was sitting here in sunny Florida listening the night the punk kid came to get me."

"Listening to what?"

Brown leered at her. "We were doing it on the phone . . . you know, getting it on. Absence makes the fond grow harder. You ever had sex with Ma Bell?"

She said nothing.

"Back in Miami Chappell was getting it all on tape. And when it was over, his little brother came to the door. You know what happened next."

She stared at the thin material in the worn cotton T-shirt he wore over a pair of khaki pants, the white nylon socks on his feet. She wanted to keep him talking, but she didn't want him talking about sex— stirring up ideas.

"Why did you rip off Sly Gallanti? Didn't you know you were stealing from Frank?"

Brown frowned. Then shrugged. "Yeah, I made a mistake. I thought Gallanti was working something on his own." And grinning, said, "But look how it turned out. If it hadn't been for that mistake I wouldn't have met you."

"My lucky day," Colleen mumbled.

"You don't know how lucky. See, I'm working up an appetite, all this talk. I've got an idea too. I'll go get breakfast, come back, and we can make some phone calls together. We'll call Craig Chappell, talk dirty to him for old time's sake. You can get into that, can't you? A little toot, maybe that'll loosen you up."

The beach was empty. A few old people out for an early-morning swim. Sly walked along the sand, glad to be out of that room, getting some fresh air. Some time alone to think. Up ahead he could see a figure sitting on the cement wall dividing the street from the beach. Right near the public rest rooms. Sly quickened his pace. Adrenaline pumped through his old heart, a welcome sign.

Walking by the wall he slowed down, eyed the guy in jeans and a raggedy T-shirt who sat, elbows on knees, chin on clenched fists.

Sly leaned against the wall. Made eye contact with the guy, who raised three fingers before getting up and walking into the men's room.

Sly followed, three tens folded in his hand. Inside, the place was empty; there were some changing stalls and a row of urinals along one wall. No sign of the mark. At one end of the building there was a cinder-block wall. Sly stepped around it. The guy was sitting on the toilet, head waist high, eyeing Sly as he came around the wall. Sly handed him the three tens and unzipped.

He was about to get into it, feeling it, giving a little circular motion of the hips, feeling the sap begin to rise, when a voice behind him said, "Well, Jesus H. Christ, what have we got here?"

Sly turned and stared at a guy in uniform.

Craig sat in Sly's hotel room, Julius propped on the bed, chain-smoking Camels, the TV on. Julius seemed to stare at it without really watching as three contestants competed for cash prizes on *Jeopardy*. The sound was turned down, so there was only the color picture, the emcee's expression showing whether the somber contestants had come up with the correct question or not.

Sly hadn't come back from his walk. Craig would look at the TV for a while, then go stare out the window. Waiting. He must have called Jeannie's apartment a hundred times, but there was no answer. He didn't expect one. He had called Ellie Schumacher and asked her to call all the car rental agencies in the Miami area to see if Brown or Jeannie had rented a car the last couple of days. It had been a long shot.

Julius said, "There's nothing we can do, huh?" It was the third or fourth time he'd asked the question, always wording it a little differently, but always getting the same answer. "I thought you were in the business of finding people."

It was the first time there had been an overtone of criticism from Julius.

"I've got to have something to go on," Craig said. "Right now there's nothing." An open pack of cigarettes was on the bed. Julius always kept the inner foil intact, never tearing it when he opened a new pack, and always refolding it when he had taken a cigarette. Now the foil was open, exposing the cigarettes.

"I thought you guys made things happen; that's how you did it."

"Yeah, under normal circumstances I could have called the police and gotten an investigation going."

"I'll tell you something," Julius said. "I don't know why we have to protect Frank. All we've got to do is find Colleen."

"All we've got to do is keep her alive." Craig reached over and picked up the pack of Camels, idly tearing off the foil lining.

"Ouch," Julius said, "my foreskin."

Craig smiled, thinking, yeah, that's what you get for your harassment. Then remembered that Julius was Jewish.

The phone rang. Julius answered it and passed it to Craig. It was Ellie Schumacher.

"Jeannie Exeter rented an '87 Jeep Cherokee from an agency over on Le Jeune."

"You're wonderful, sweetheart. I'll bet you've got a tag number too."

"And the color and model number." She repeated it while Craig wrote the numbers down. "Anything else you need?"

"Just stay by the phone in case I need you."

"I'm not going anywhere," Ellie said. She hung up.

Craig told Julius what Ellie had found. "Now we've got something to go on," he said.

"Yeah," Julius said, "the famous needle . . ."

Half an hour later the phone rang again. This time Julius listened for a while, his face downcast, resting against his thumb, while the two fingers of his right hand pointed upward in a V that held a cigarette. Smoke swirled around his head as he cradled the phone to his ear with the other hand.

After a moment Julius said, "Anything happens to her, Johnny, and you're going to bring a lot of trouble on yourself. More trouble than you've already got."

And handed the phone to Craig, saying, "He wants to talk to you."

Craig took the phone and said, "It's time to meet, Johnny."

Brown laughed. "You think so, cowboy," he said. "I want you to hear something first."

Craig could hear the phone being placed down and some movement. Then a muffled sound, like someone sobbing, or gagging. And Brown's voice in the distance. "Yeah, sweet thing, that feel good? You like that?"

Craig gripped the phone like it was prey, his knuckles turning white. He said, "Brown!"

There was the sound of Brown's laughter and more stifled cries. Then Brown came back. "Remind you of old times? Get you excited, cowboy? I seem to remember that you like listening to people make it on the phone."

"Listen to me, Brown—"

"She likes it, will take it anywhere. Of course she hasn't got much choice, tied up and gagged."

"Brown, talk to me!"

Brown laughed again. "Okay, that's what you want, cowboy. Frank's going to get you the money today. You drive out the Tamiami Trail with it. There's an old gas station and general store along there about an hour this side of Naples. You can't miss it. There's a couple of phones outside. You'll get another call at midnight. Make sure you're alone, cowboy, or sweet thing here will get hurt."

Frank called. "What're you, making book out of there? I've been trying to call for the past hour."

"Things are getting busy," Julius said.

"They're going to get busier. I'm coming in on the noon flight then going straight to the bank where I've made arrangements for money to be transferred. After that we're going after Brown."

"Frank, I—"

"Just be at the hotel," Frank said. "I've got enough problems. I don't want to have to chase you down too."

"Frank—"

But Frank had hung up.

Twenty-two

*F*RANK BISHOP REMINDED CRAIG OF AN OLD-TIME FIGHT manager. The guy came into the room talking, cocky, never still, never really looking at anyone. A bellhop came in behind him with two suitcases and set them on the floor. Frank gave him a dollar and the kid backed out of the room.

Julius had said to Craig, "He studied for the priesthood once. As he gets older I think he thinks he made it. In fact he may be a monsignor by now. Bishop Bishop."

Craig stuck with his own impression. In part because he had a hard time connecting Colleen's white-haired stepfather with any form of holiness.

"Julie, whoever thought it would come to this? What have you heard from her?" Bishop ignored Craig as he moved around the room, waving his arms, glancing at Julius, who sat on the bed, smoking.

"She's with Brown. That's all you need to know, isn't it? Frank, this is—"

"Where's Sly?"

"Went out this morning and hasn't been back. Frank, this is Craig Chappell."

Bishop stopped walking, rubbed his hands together, his back to Craig, the shoulders rounded. In that moment, yeah, he could see where the priest image came from.

Bishop said, "You didn't tell me, Julie."

"What was I supposed to tell you? He's been in this thing from the beginning, you knew that."

Frank turned, his hands clasped together, glanced at Craig, then back to Julius. Craig sat in a chair next to the window overlooking a small pool, thinking of Colleen and Frank. A twelve-year-old girl having to sleep locked in the bathroom to escape her father.

Julius, the real father, saying, "Brown wants him to deliver. Don't forget that you started this war, Frank."

"Where is he?" Frank asked Julius.

"Brown? We don't know. He wants Chappell to bring the money to a place out in the Everglades and wait for a phone call."

"We'll all go," Frank said.

"Not if you want to see Colleen again, you won't." Craig stood up. "You don't like it, but right now I'm all you've got."

Julius said, "Listen to him, Frank. He knows what he's doing. It's his business."

"I know what his business is," Frank snapped. "Carl's dead."

"I couldn't do anything about that," Craig said. "I can do something to save Colleen, though, but I've got to get started." He had wanted to leave after Brown called, standing there listening to Colleen's muffled cries. But he had to wait for Bishop and the money. During that time he'd been able at least to set up a rental car. Now he could go—if Frank gave his blessing.

Frank hesitated, turned, raised his hands to Julius.

"Go with it," Julius said.

Frank turned back to Craig. "There's half a million dollars in the large suitcase there. I want it back. I want the stuff Brown stole from Sly, and I want Colleen."

"In that order?" Craig asked.

"I don't care what order. When I leave here I want it with me on that plane back to New York."

"What about Brown?"

"Kill him."

Craig smiled. "A few weeks ago it was the other way around. What were you paying Brown for his contract on me?"

"It doesn't matter."

"It does to me. Julius just told you, this is my business. And I'm used to getting paid for it."

Frank sighed. "Listen, if you don't kill Brown, he's going to kill you."

"He's been trying. I'll take my chances. How much?"

Frank hesitated again, turned his back to Craig and said, "Twenty-five grand."

"You can do better than that. I'm walking out of here with five hundred grand. There's nothing to stop me if I decide to just keep walking."

John Leslie

Julius said to Frank, "He won't do that. He won't leave Colleen with that asshole."

"How do you know what he'll do?" Frank asked.

"I know," Julius said. "You know you can trust me, and I say you can trust him."

"Wherever that suitcase goes, I'm going," Frank said. "I'll take my chances with Brown."

"So will Colleen," Craig said, "but if that's the way you want it, you find your own transportation. I don't want you anywhere near me. And I want fifty grand, half up front, which was what Brown was worth when he was in Montreal. I figure he's doubled in value since then. Besides, I've got a life to piece back together which you tried to destroy."

"Dear God," Frank said.

Julius said, "Craig, let me have a word with him alone."

Craig nodded and went out into the hall. All of this was taking time; he wanted to get going.

Julius said, "Why didn't you tell me Colleen tried to kill herself?"

Frank hadn't stopped moving or talking since Craig left. He walked around the room, stood for a moment looking out the window, then went into the bathroom and stood at the mirror. Julius could see him running his fingers through his white hair. The question didn't seem to bother him. "It's history, the past. I don't deal in the past. The secret to this life is you don't stop to mourn what you can't change. Carl's dead. It was a deep blow, but I've kept going."

"You should have told me."

"You're too emotional. I didn't want to upset you. I left it to Colleen to tell you about it if she wanted to."

"She didn't tell me. Craig did."

212

Frank came and stood in the doorway to the bathroom. "How did he know?"

"She told him."

Frank shook his head. "This is what I can't understand. Why has Colleen taken such an interest in the guy?"

"Maybe it's a boy-girl thing," Julius said. "It happens, you know."

"No. It isn't going to happen. I couldn't live with that. When I think about Carl in Montreal . . . no, it isn't going to happen." He came into the room. "I don't trust him, Julie. I don't care what you say."

"He'll find Colleen. I know you can trust him to do that."

"But he doesn't get the suitcase," Frank said. "I'm not taking any more chances with this guy. I've got a car downstairs; we're going to be right on his tail."

Julius saw there was no point arguing. Frank's mind was made up.

Julius in the lobby said, "Go on. Get on your way. But we're going to be right behind you."

"I'm not going to let that crazy son of a bitch get us all killed. If I have to, I'll kill him," Craig said. He meant it. He didn't like the sanctimonious Frank Bishop. Another one of those guys who had had his own way in life and had done nothing but make a mess of other people's lives. Colleen's. Carl's. With a good start on Craig's.

"I'll try to keep control of him," Julius said.

"Then you better have a gun."

"Sly's got one in the room. I'll take it."

"Where the hell do you think he is?"

As if he'd just been waiting for somebody to ask, Sly walked through the double doors of the hotel. Right up to them. A cockeyed smile on his lips.

213

"What happened?" Julius asked him.

"I ran into a problem over on the beach."

"Jesus. The same thing again?"

For a seventy-year-old man, Sly still managed to look sheepish, Craig thought.

"Not quite the same thing," Sly said. "A vice cop picked me up. In the men's room."

"Getting your shank cleaned?"

"Something like that. I had to spend some time in the station answering questions. I think they looked me up on their computer and thought maybe they'd hauled in a big fish. Wanted to know what I was doing down here."

"What did you tell them?"

"That after twenty years I thought I deserved a vacation."

"You didn't mention Frank, say anything at all about what's going on here?" Craig asked.

"I didn't even think about it, in case they've got a computer that reads minds," Sly said.

Craig nodded. "I'm taking off," he said to Julius. "When you get to that rundown old gas station, go in and have a beer, listen to the Florida crackers. Sooner or later I'll be in. And keep Frank quiet."

"What have I missed?" Sly asked.

"Julius will fill you in," Craig said.

Hurtling across the Tamiami Trail, Craig thought about Julius. The guy had sat in the hotel, worrying about Colleen, chain-smoking cigarettes. Craig had tried to get him to talk, get his mind off this for a while, and Julius had told him about the roulette system he wanted to try out if he could ever get a big enough bankroll together. That had been the idea behind the book on Lansky.

Julius explained the system in detail—a staking system that relied on his ability to keep track of his wins and losses. He would bet only on high-low, odd-even, or red-black combinations—not the numbers. On a note pad he would write down a frame of five numbers—like five ones, if he were betting a dollar. Each time he won he crossed out a one and bet another dollar; each time he lost he wrote the amount lost to his row of numbers, added the two outside numbers together and bet that amount. Each time he closed out a frame of numbers it meant a profit. But it was when he was losing that he needed the bankroll behind him, until eventually the system closed itself out with a profit, which, he said, it always would—provided there was a sufficient stake behind him.

Half a million dollars would be quite a stake, Craig thought. He'd like to see Julius get his hands on some of it and go to the Bahamas where he could have a last fling.

He tried to picture the immediate future. He kept seeing John Brown and Frank Bishop, seeing them face off against each other, surprised. It was a kind of solution, and Craig knew he was daydreaming, putting the script together the way he would like to see it, but he couldn't see it happening that way in reality. Still, it was a nice thought. But just suppose it could be managed, then what? What came after for Colleen, Sly, and Julius? And himself? That got pretty murky.

He gave up and decided to concentrate on the present—finding Brown before midnight. It was three o'clock. There was a lot of wilderness to comb in the next nine hours. . . .

Brown said he had to go out for a while. He didn't want anybody coming around, looking in windows, so

215

he was going to have to put her back in the trunk. But he said he wouldn't be gone long. He untied her from the bed.

He patted her hand, said, Okay, now, okay. Said, Everything was all right. Said she would be all right. She said, Why are you being nice to me?

"'Cause I'm your friend," Brown said. "I'm going to take care of you. That's why you have to go back in the trunk—where it's safe."

"Okay," she said. She felt things, lots of things, but she didn't think about them. The humiliation was gone. The pain was gone. The fear and anger were even gone. In place of that was a deep hatred, unlike any feeling she had ever known. There was such a quiet intensity to it that she was unsure if she might not suddenly go crazy, do something crazy.

She was almost happy to be back inside the trunk. It was dark in here. No one would see her. No one could hurt her. She would be safe, left alone. She wanted to be left alone. And she never, never, ever wanted to be raped again in her life.

_____ *Twenty-three*

*T*HE TAMIAMI TRAIL SPLIT THE WILDERNESS OF THE Everglades with razorlike precision. The road stretched out of Miami with barely a bend or grade, flat and straight as a stretched rubber band. And just about as tense, Craig thought. He was driving west, into the sun. On either side of the two-lane highway, as far as he could see, sawgrass rustled like a prairie wheat field before harvest. In the distance jagged palm fronds were etched against the sky while birds whirled and rode the air currents. In the deep grass along the canals and swamp rivers, he imagined alligators lying in sullen wait for their prey.

The way Brown would be waiting for him.

He had passed the large modern gas station with its convenience store just before the intersection with Route 27 that wound north to Lake Okeechobee. There was the Miccosukee Indian reservation and trading post, the turnoff to the Everglades State Park at Shark River, and then nothing: endless miles of swamp.

Where would Brown hole up? If he had some cabin tucked back in here, it could take days, even weeks to track him down, and there was always the possibility that he'd never be found. Outside of Miami and the swamp, there was no civilized place out here until you got to Marco Island, or Naples.

Except for Everglades City, Craig had looked at a map before leaving. Everglades City was the closest place in the area to the old gas station. Less than an hour's drive from where he was supposed to get his midnight phone call.

He'd crossed the Tamiami Trail maybe twice, three times since he'd been in Florida. Once to go back to Marco Island where his father had brought him tarpon fishing years ago, when he was twelve or thirteen. They'd stayed in the old Marco Island Inn, a sprawling frame hotel on the edge of town. Marco Island then was nothing more than a fishing camp stuck bang in the middle of the mangroves on the Gulf.

Craig had brought Barry there a few years ago and found it worse than Key West. He couldn't believe it. All those mangroves were now condos. High rises. You got in them and looked out, you could have been on Lake Shore Drive in Chicago looking over Lake

Michigan. The only thing recognizable was the Marco Island Inn where Craig took Barry.

In the foyer glass cases hung on the walls, containing tarpon scales tacked onto corkboard, all dated and signed, going back to the early 1900s. They looked like medals, silver medallions beaten thin.

Barry must have gone through them all one evening before Craig had come over to join him in the bar. When Craig walked in the door, Barry had his finger on one of the glass cases, pointing to a tarpon scale singled out from the rest that had Craig Chappell's name, the date, 1960, and the weight of the tarpon it had come from, sixty-nine pounds.

It had excited Barry to find it—a piece of the past, some family history.

Remembering that now, Craig thought what it would be like to pin Brown up. Hang him out to dry, so to speak, from one of those palm trees in the swamp. With Barry's name and the date of his death scratched in Brown's skull.

Everglades City seemed as good as any place to begin looking.

What if the cowboy showed up here? Brown believed he would. There was still lots of time before midnight, still plenty of light left for tracking. The bounty hunter, Brown was sure, would take advantage of that, would prowl around the area asking questions, looking at room reservations—maybe even looking for a Jeep Cherokee if he had been smart enough to check the rental agencies in Miami.

Brown figured he was safe enough, tucked back here in the fishing camp, the Jeep parked off the road behind the cabin which he'd signed for under a different name. He could sit here and watch for him.

Brown could see the office from his cabin, if the cowboy went in there, and anybody driving by the road in front. But he wasn't sure he wanted to be sitting here.

Just in case, he'd driven into Naples that morning after making his calls and purchased a car phone which he'd had installed in the Jeep. He was back at the cabin at noon, less than three hours after he'd left.

The girl worried him. She was in the trunk, hugging her body and sucking her thumb when he opened the top. She wouldn't say anything, just looked at him once and then closed her eyes. He touched her, poked her leg with his finger, but she seemed to go deeper into herself. Jesus, man. What was he supposed to do with her? She was like a zombie. He had to get her out of there, get her dressed. He didn't want to hurt her; she wasn't any good to him dead, but he wanted her able to move.

"Hey," he said. "Come on. Let's get you dressed."

She didn't move.

He took her arm, tried to drag her up. She was rigid, holding herself, her eyes still closed. "Come on," he said. "We're going bye-bye."

She opened her eyes. Took her thumb out of her mouth and said in a tiny baby voice, "Where?"

It was three-thirty when he got to the old frame building with its twin gas pumps and a piece of plywood propped up that advertised BAIT in big black letters. And another sign beside it that said: MARRIAGES PERFORMED HERE.

Craig made a left turn off the Tamiami Trail into the dirt parking area and pulled up in front of the pumps. He put one of the nozzles in his tank, set the clip on the handle to pump the gas while he walked around. He found the phones where Brown said they would be. He looked down a side road that seemed to lead back into the swamp off the main road, its narrow, pitted asphalt surface shaded and dark beneath the thick growth of mangroves and overhanging foliage that bordered the road. He walked back to the car and squeezed in an even ten dollars worth of gas. Then went into the store.

Two older men in overalls and a lumpy blond woman in pink shorts and a sleeveless blouse sat on swivel stools at a long counter. They drank Budweiser from long-neck bottles. The men told jokes, and Craig recognized the nasal accents of a couple of Florida crackers.

He stood at the cash register down the counter from them. The lumpy blond got up from her stool, went behind the counter and came down to him. "Can I he'p you?" she said.

"I'm looking for a guy, supposed to meet me here," Craig said. He described John Brown.

The woman listened, then shouted the description down to the men she'd been sitting with. They both shook their heads. "Well, if he comes in, don't tell him I was here. I want to surprise him." Craig put a ten dollar bill on the counter and left.

Everglades City. There were a couple hotels, a marina, the Rod and Gun Club where Presidents had stayed, an alligator pit where you could pay to see a guy climb in there with the grinning reptiles and tussle with them, sit on them while he held their jaws open.

Craig stopped at the hotels and asked about Brown. No one recognized the description. He described Colleen. No, no one had seen her. What about a black Jeep Cherokee? The hotel clerks looked at Craig like he was crazy, like what did he think they did all day, sit in the window watching traffic go by?

He went to the Rod and Gun Club and got the same response. Checked in the restaurants, a convenience store that seemed to be the only grocery store in this burg. It was a fishing town. Commercial fishermen came in wearing their white rubber boots, talking about their last catch, that same cracker accent Craig had heard back at the gas station. Red-neck country.

It was five o'clock. He decided to drive around, make one sweep around the place, see if he could spot the Jeep before going on. Lobster and stone-crab traps were stacked around many of the houses where pickup trucks and a few Jeeps were parked—none black with the tag number Ellie Schumacher had given him.

He followed a road that curved out along the water, a wide channel, more like a river coursing between mangrove islands. After half a mile he came by a fishing camp that advertised cabins for rent and a free boat ramp.

Craig stopped and went into the office, where he gave his description to an elderly woman in jeans and a blue work shirt, waiting for her to shake her head negatively. Instead she said, "Yes, that sounds like the man in cabin five."

"Driving a black Jeep, have a young woman in her early twenties with him?"

"Yes, the Jeep's right, I didn't see anyone with him, though," the woman said. "But he left earlier this afternoon and I don't think he's come back, although the cabin's paid up through tonight."

Julius looked at his watch as Frank turned the car off the Tamiami Trail, stopping at the dilapidated house where gas was sold and marriages performed. It was ten after six. In the trunk was half a million dollars in hundred dollar bills stacked in a suitcase.

"Who would get married in a dump like this?" Frank asked.

Sly had opened the back door of the sedan. "Somebody in a hurry," he said. "A shotgun in his back."

"Nobody does that anymore," Frank said. "You're living in the past."

"Don't believe it," Julius said. "You left the city behind. This is catfish and hush-puppy land. They stick to the old ways."

The three of them got out of the car, walked into the store and took seats at the counter.

"Where's Chappell?" Frank asked, looking around. A couple farmers and a blonde-floozy type were sitting down the counter from them, drinking beer.

"He said he'd be here," Julius said. "He didn't say when."

One of the guys down the counter said to the blonde, "Mary, looks like we got three live ones with money to burn. Fix 'em up."

She was thinking how hungry she was, wondering what time it was—she couldn't remember eating last—when Brown stopped. She heard the Jeep door slam, and a few minutes later he came back and they drove for a while. She seemed to have lost her sense of time. Had she been in here an hour, two, three? The air was stale. She remembered him punching some holes in the trunk, but breathing was still difficult. It seemed like they drove for only a little while, though, before Brown stopped again. She waited for the door to slam but the next thing she heard he was in the back, fumbling with the latch on the trunk. She put her thumb in her mouth.

"I got you a sandwich," he said. "And some coffee if you want it."

She wanted it. But she didn't want to appear eager. Since she'd retreated into herself, Brown had relented. He seemed uneasy around her now, like he wasn't prepared for this situation: he could only intimidate someone who was frightened, who had something to lose. How was he supposed to know that he'd taken hostage a woman who had once tried to kill herself? Even though now more than ever she wanted to live.

She let him put his hand under her neck, pull her up in the trunk. He held the coffee for her while she sipped it, and he said, "See, Johnny B. ain't such a bad guy. He will treat you right."

She wanted to spill the coffee down his crotch, but it wasn't hot enough. She kept her eyes down. He opened the cellophane on a convenience-store ham and cheese sandwich. She took a bite, wanting to devour it, but forced herself to eat slowly, chewing deliberately, not looking at Brown.

He said, "Now you promise to be good, you can stay out here. I've got to tie you up, but I won't put you back in the trunk. You promise?" Like a little kid.

She said, "What time is it?"

"Nine o'clock," Brown said.

Craig drove around, came back by the fishing camp several times after having looked in the windows of cabin 5 earlier. He could see the unmade bed, but there was nothing else to indicate anyone would be back.

It had been dark for an hour or so when he made the decision to leave Everglades City, some instinct telling him Brown wouldn't return here. So it was back on the Tamiami Trail, east this time, to wait for the midnight call.

It was eight-thirty when he got back to the gas station. He went inside and found the three old mafiosi sitting at the counter. The blonde was still sitting at the far end, keeping company with only one of the crackers now, who still sat sipping beer.

When Craig joined the old men, the blonde came down and said, "I thought maybe they was gettin' married and the women stood 'em up." She laughed. "I've seen it happen in here the other way around enough times."

"Coffee," Craig said.

She put a cup in front of him, saying, "We close at nine." Then shuffled back to her man, a pair of fuzzy pink bedroom slippers on her feet, Craig noticed.

"Any sign of Brown?" Sly asked.

"He was staying in a place not far from here, but he hasn't been back there for half a day, and it doesn't look like he's going back," Craig said.

"Colleen," Julius said. A cigarette in his hand, with close to a pack of butts stubbed out in the ashtray in front of him.

"Nobody's seen her."

Frank wouldn't look at Craig. Staring at the wall behind the counter, Frank said, "I'm going along on the delivery tonight, in case you need some time to get used to the idea."

Craig said, "It's an idea I can live with. To tell you the truth, I had about the same idea a little earlier today."

_____ *Twenty-four*

BROWN WAS PARKED IN ONE OF THE MANGROVE-shrouded cutoffs along the old road, a mile from the place where Chappell would now be waiting for the phone call. Ten minutes before midnight. A perfect night, no moon, no traffic back here. For the past couple hours he'd kept Colleen in the back, but not in the trunk, her hands tied. She wouldn't talk, but she'd eaten and she seemed calmer. Now she was locked back in the trunk.

In another half hour he was going to have half a million dollars of Frank Bishop's money. Frank would have his daughter back and a dead cowboy. That was worth half a million dollars, Brown figured. He would disappear into the swamp and later quietly take a boat over to the Bahamas. Invest the money, live off the interest, maybe get him a little business going over there. Or buy his own island. All kinds of possibilities when you had half a million in cash.

But first he was going to have to get by Bishop. The little guy would try something, Brown was sure. But as long as Brown had Colleen, Frank wasn't going to risk losing another child. Brown decided to keep that advantage until he was sure he was clear.

They waited side by side in separate cars, Frank and Julius sitting in the Lincoln Town Car Frank had rented. Sly was with Craig in the Ford hatchback. The gas station was closed, the traffic along the highway light.

"You got a gun?" Sly asked.

Craig nodded. He reached under the seat and took out the snubnosed .38 he'd gotten from his office. "What about Frank? Is he carrying?"

"I don't know," Sly said. "Probably, but he isn't talking much to me. He's still convinced we're running some scam against him. You're taking a chance letting him go along on this."

"Maybe," Craig said. "But it's a chance I'm willing to take."

Two cars passed fifty yards away on the Tamiami Trail. When the noise receded he could hear the night sounds again—tree frogs croaking, some crickets. It reminded him of summers back in New Jersey when he was a kid.

"I've got a nine-millimeter Browning automatic," Sly said. "It might be easier to use with only one hand. Or if you want any backup—"

"You and Julius stay out of this. I'm going to have enough on my hands with Frank. I don't want to worry about you two."

Sly grinned at him in the dark. "You think this is something new to me? Come on. Two, three times a week I sometimes went through this in New York. You're not talking to an amateur."

Craig thought, yeah, and you get mugged in the park by a kid and picked up by vice on the beach. He said, "This isn't New York."

"Same story, different time, different place," Sly said. "But it's your show. You call the shots."

"No," Craig said. "For now, Brown does."

Julius said, "When I see her I'm going to tell her."

"Tell her what?" Frank demanded. They sat in the luxury car with the windows up, the air conditioner going, Frank still in the dark suit and tie he'd arrived in from New York.

"I should have done it a long time ago. I'm her father. She's an adult. She's been through a lot, Frank, and she has a right to know that."

Frank was silent a moment. "Over my dead body," he said.

"Don't ask me to make that decision," Julius said.

The phone rang. Craig looked at his watch as he got out of the car. Midnight. On the second ring he picked up the receiver.

"Not bad, cowboy. I was hoping you'd get it on the first ring."

"I'm listening," Craig said. "Talk to me."

"Atta boy, you listen real good, because if there's any fuck-up, the girl's the first to go."

"Let's get it over with."

"Where you're standin', right behind you, there's a

road comes off the Tamiami Trail, goes south back into the 'glades."

"I see it."

"Get in your car and set your odometer. Drive fifteen-point-four miles along that road and stop. You better be alone. You got that, cowboy?"

"I've got a broken arm but my brain's working just fine. Keep talking."

"What are you driving?"

"A Ford hatchback."

"As soon as you park, take your clothes off, get out and stand by your car. When I see you, if you've even got socks on, your brain's gonna be shut down for good."

"I'm wearing a cast."

"I know that . . . I don't want to see anything else. What's the money in?"

"A suitcase."

"When you see my lights flash twice bring it to the middle of the road and open it up where I can see it. Then you get back in the car and drive."

"What about Colleen?"

"You're going to be in wide-open country, swampland where you can see for maybe two miles before the road curves. You drive for one mile and stop. She'll walk out and meet you."

"How do I know you'll keep your word?"

Brown laughed. "You don't, cowboy, but we're doing this my way. So take it or leave it."

Craig hesitated, trying to buy some time, find an angle. But Brown said, "It's now or never," and hung up.

Craig walked up to the driver's side of the Lincoln, where Frank sat with his window half down. Craig said, "Get the money; we're going."

Frank touched a button and the trunk opened. He

got out of the car and Craig followed him to the back. "I want to see what's in that suitcase," Craig said.

"You think I've got newspaper cut up in there?"

"I'm going to be alone with the guy when it's opened. I don't want any surprises."

Frank raised the trunk lid, reached in and snapped open the suitcase. The money was there. And on top of it a pump-action sawed-off shotgun. Frank picked it up. Craig could see himself standing buck naked in the middle of the road caught in a crossfire.

Julius and Sly were out of the cars, standing at the back of the Lincoln. "Where's it going to happen?" Julius asked.

"Fifteen miles down that road."

"We can give you a five- or ten-minute lead. Then come in and back you up."

Craig shook his head. "Brown's already thought of that. We're going to be right in the swamp, in the open. He's probably back there now. He sees me, and you coming in later, Colleen doesn't stand a chance."

"They got telephones in the swamp?" Julius asked.

"I wondered about that. Maybe he's got a phone in the Jeep. It doesn't matter. I'm going in alone."

Frank said, "Not quite." He picked up the shotgun and got in the backseat of the Ford while Craig opened the hatchback and put the suitcase inside. He closed the trunk.

Sly was standing beside him, holding the nine-millimeter by the barrel. "Take it," he said. "It may be faster if you have to use it. I'll trade you the snubbie for it."

From his mangrove cover Brown watched the Ford go by, doing thirty-five, forty over the potholed road. Silhouetted in the dash lights he could see the cowboy driving, but no sidekick riding shotgun. Which didn't mean somebody couldn't be crouched down in the back or lying in the trunk. Brown waited for ten minutes, giving another car a chance to follow the guy in if Chappell was stupid enough to have set that up. When nothing came by, Brown eased onto the asphalt and drove slowly without lights.

Sly and Julius sat in the Lincoln, Julius behind the wheel, Sly next to him. "What are we going to do, just sit here?" Sly asked.

"I'm open to suggestions," Julius said. His heart was pounding; he'd had to empty the ashtray twice.

Sly looked at his watch. "He's been gone twenty minutes. I say we follow him. We can go in slow, no lights. It's fifteen miles. We can at least get a little closer than this, be there just in case."

Julius reached down and turned the key in the ignition.

Frank, crouched on the floor between the front and back seats, said, "Take it easy. You trying to hit every bump in the road?"

Craig slowed down but didn't say anything.

Frank said, "Colleen claims you didn't kill Carl, Brown did."

"You should listen to her. She knows what she's talking about."

"But if you hadn't been up there in the first place, it wouldn't have happened."

"Listen," Craig said, talking over his shoulder, trying to steer to avoid potholes. "Brown didn't have to shoot Carl, he didn't have to kill anybody—except that's what he does, he kills people. He worked for you, remember?"

He watched the odometer roll over to the fourteen-mile mark. They were on a long straight stretch of road now in much better condition than the jarring miles he'd just driven. The high beam of his headlights spread over the road and a sea of high grass that drifted into the darkness. Fifteen miles on the odometer. He began to slow down at point three, and came to a stop at fifteen point four. He turned off the lights and killed the engine. Wrapped in darkness, hearing only the rustle of the dry grass, the insects, he began to undress. He released the catch on the hatchback, then opened his door and, totally naked, stepped outside. He reached in under the seat and slipped Sly's nine-millimeter into the sling supporting his cast and felt ridiculous standing there without his clothes. He listened, thought he heard the sound of a car, and waited . . .

Definitely a vehicle approaching, the noise louder now, a higher-revved engine than a car, more like the sound of a Jeep.

Brown saw him standing there, his arm up in the blue sling, his naked body white against the headlights. He stopped and let the Jeep idle twenty-five yards back from the car sitting there with its hatchback open. He picked up the .45 lying on the passenger's seat and opened the door. He had removed the bulb from the interior light. Then flicked his lights twice, down on low and back on high beam before stepping outside the Jeep, using the door as a shield, resting the gun on the open window.

Brown watched as the cowboy walked to the back of the Ford, extended the hatchback and pulled out the suitcase, and carried the bag toward the Jeep where he set it down in the center of the road halfway between the Jeep and the car. Reached down and undid the clasps and pulled the top up.

Brown saw the money, banded and stacked in piles. Watched as the cowboy stood up, looked into the glare of the Jeep headlights and stepped away from the suitcase.

Brown sighted down the long barrel, aiming just above the guy's sling, and as he was about to pull the trigger saw a glint of metal from over the backseat of the Ford . . .

Craig saw it too, as he was turning, and threw himself backwards to the side of the narrow road, his body scraping against asphalt as he rolled into the tall, bottom-soggy, knife-edged sawgrass just as the shotgun blasted and Brown opened fire.

Craig pulled himself through the grass back out of the sidestream of light spread by the Jeep's headlights. The shotgun roared once more and glass shattered. Then he heard the ping of a bullet striking metal just before the Ford exploded, and in seconds the rental car was totally enveloped in flame.

Frank Bishop was slowly being cremated, but Craig doubted his soul would ever make it to heaven.

He had taken the sling strap from around his neck and dumped the automatic out, holding it in his left hand, pulling himself through the swamp back toward the road and the Jeep. Brown was still crouched behind the door. Craig aimed the automatic and pulled the trigger; nothing happened—the damned thing was water-logged, and jammed. Fucking automatics.

Brown looked into the swamp, then back at the burning car. Small explosions of glass and metal kicked flames onto the road that spit and burned into the asphalt. Any one of them touched that suitcase, Craig thought, $500,000 would go up in smoke.

John Leslie

Brown must have been thinking the same thing because he left the cover of the Jeep door and ran in a crouch toward the suitcase fifteen yards away.

Craig was about half that distance from the Jeep, but he had to wait until Brown had his back to him before he could even get to his feet. Craig sprinted across the road as Brown got to the money and bent down to close the case. Craig, bleeding, wet, climbed into the cab and slipped back behind the driver's seat. A steamer trunk was on the floor beside him.

Brown got in and shoved the suitcase in behind the passenger's seat. Craig held his breath. Brown banged the door closed and put the Jeep in gear, reversing, turning around, finally heading back the way they'd come.

Craig raised up and put the barrel of the automatic in the small hollow where Brown's head and neck joined.

"The party's still going," Craig said. "Slowly now, pass your gun back here."

Brown handed the .45 over his shoulder. Craig took it in his right hand, then exchanged the automatic.

"Where is she?"

"You didn't follow instructions," Brown said.

"I've got a little voice in my head telling me to pull the trigger," Craig said. "That's an instruction I would like to follow. Now where is she?"

Brown didn't say. Headlights from an oncoming car suddenly flashed in the windshield and Brown stepped on the gas, crashing head-on into the Lincoln Town Car.

_____ *Twenty-five*

_T_HEY SAW THE FIRE THROUGH THE MANGROVE TREES.
Yellow and blue flames licking the night sky. Julius
said, "Time to move." And pulled the full headlights
on instead of the parking lights they'd been inching
along under. "Jesus," Sly said, "let's go."

Moments later they came to a curve. The trees
began to thin, and as they came around it, there was
another vehicle coming straight for them on the
narrow road, no place for the wide Lincoln to go, and
no time to go there anyway. Julius braked, trying to
pull over as far as he could, blinded by the lights. The

Jeep, he could see it now, slammed into their front grill, the big, heavy Lincoln absorbing the shock.

Julius felt like somebody had pulled a chair out from under him as he was sitting down, a kind of sinking feeling with some added pressure, a warm tightening around his chest. Like a bad case of heartburn. Thinking, Jesus, was this a heart attack? "You all right?" he asked Sly, his voice sounding distant.

"Yeah, fine," Sly said. "I didn't know they made cars like this anymore, almost as solid as the old Packards."

"Where's the gun?"

"I've got it right here in my hand."

"Somebody's getting out of the Jeep." Julius wasn't sure he could move right away. He wanted to just sit here, see what was happening to him. The guy in the Jeep seemed to stagger, bent over.

"I've got him covered," Sly said. The window was down, he was leaning out, pointing the gun toward the Jeep. "You see who it is?"

"I can't see worth a damn at night," Julius said.

"You were driving!"

"I didn't trust you to. Besides, we were going slow."

"He's got Frank's suitcase."

"Then go after him." The pressure on his chest was lifting.

Julius could see the guy walking away from the wreck now, heading toward the swamp, dragging the suitcase along. Sly was out of the car. Julius pushed his door open and got out, relieved he was able to move. Sly had gone into the swamp after Brown, if it was Brown, but it was too dark to see them.

Julius walked to the Jeep, looked in through the open passenger door and heard someone moan. Julius got inside. Saw Craig lying in back, the cast on his arm, no clothes on, his head up against an old trunk.

"Hey," Julius said. "Wake up." He got into the back, put his hand on Craig's head.

Craig moaned again, said, "What happened?"

"You were in a wreck, ran into a Lincoln Town Car. You must have banged your head."

Craig sat up. "Where is Brown?"

"Trying to cross the swamp with a suitcase, but Sly's gone after him. Where's Frank? . . . You didn't get Colleen?"

Craig was up running his hands over the floor of the Jeep. He picked up a gun wedged between the back door and the trunk. "Frank's dead," Craig said. "Brown shot the gas tank out on the Ford. Frank was inside."

Julius felt the warm vise begin to grip his chest again. He'd known Frank too many years not to feel some sorrow, even if the guy was a bastard. But Colleen was still missing . . .

"Brown's probably got Sly's automatic. The thing jammed on me. Has Sly got my gun?"

"Yeah, he'll bring him back. Brown seemed to be hurt. What's in the trunk?"

"I've been wondering about that," Craig said. "I think it's time to find out."

Craig opened the back doors, squeezed around the trunk and stepped out onto the road. Julius sat down inside, still feeling the pressure. "You okay?" Craig asked.

"A little heartburn."

Craig opened the trunk. They both looked inside. Colleen lay there on sacks of white powder, her hands and feet bound, a rag stuffed in her mouth, but her eyes were open. Craig took the rag out of her mouth. She gulped air. Looking down at her, Julius felt tears coming. "Colleen . . ."

Craig undid her hands and feet. She sat up slowly,

237

rubbing her wrists, then her ankles, starting to get out of the trunk.

"Take it easy," Julius said.

"I'm okay. I just want out of here. Where's Brown?"

"Coming. Sly's gone after him."

She seemed to think about that. She said, "I heard an explosion."

"My car," Craig said. "Brown torched another one."

Getting out of the trunk, she looked at him, paused, and said, almost managing a smile, "I see you dressed for the occasion."

There was movement off the road, and Sly called out from the dark: "Here he is. Not in too good a shape, but he could be worse. What do we do with him?"

Julius leaned next to Colleen and said softly, "Frank's dead."

She looked at him, didn't say anything for a moment. Then: "I guess I'm an orphan again."

Julius glanced at Craig, who winked.

Craig said, "There anything to wear in that car? Even a blanket."

"Take this guy's clothes," Sly said, pointing the .38 at Brown. "He's ruined enough of yours." Brown stood there leaning up against the side of the Jeep, a ribbon of blood staining his forehead. Hovering in the darkness, Craig thought about it. Why not?

Colleen was walking back and forth along the road, Julius walking beside her.

Brown didn't resist as Craig unbuttoned his pants, slipped them down around his ankles. Jesus, the guy was wearing skimpy red briefs. He didn't want those. Sly held the gun on him, one arm clamped around Brown's neck, while Craig pulled the khaki pants off his feet and got into them himself. They fit. With his arm in the cast he wouldn't be able to get into the T-shirt anyway. Besides, it smelled too bad.

"What are we gonna do with him?" Sly asked. "Why don't I take him back in the swamp, put a bullet in his head. What good is he?"

Brown hadn't spoken. Now he lifted his head, said, "You had your chance, faggot."

Sly jammed the barrel of the snubbie in Brown's stomach. "Maybe I'll get another one."

"We've got to get out of here. Somebody must have heard that car go up and seen the fire. I don't want to get stuck here talking to cops with a trunk full of coke and half a million dollars in a suitcase. What do you want to do with the coke?"

Sly grinned. "You kidding? That's a hundred grand in there. My future."

"Does the Lincoln run?"

"Shit," Sly said. "Maybe five hundred dollars of body work and it'll be like new."

Julius came up. "I'll get the car started."

"Pop the trunk," Craig said. "Sly can help me load it." He looked at Colleen, who was walking toward them. "Hold this gun on Brown." He handed her Brown's .45. "If he moves, shoot him. Can you do that?"

Colleen looked at Brown, no expression on her face. "I think so," she said.

"Growing up with Frank, you'd think I would know something about guns," Colleen said. She stood three feet from Brown, who still leaned against the Jeep. Sly and Craig were carrying the trunk between them, Craig with the suitcase in his other hand, walking slowly toward the Lincoln. "But this is the first time I've ever even had one in my hand."

Brown looked at her. "What are you thinking?"

"A lot of things," she said. "Why don't you run?"

"So you can shoot me?"

"You've got a chance. It'll be the only one you get. I really don't know if I can do it."

Brown stood away from the Jeep, facing her, his hands turned up, showing her how defenseless he was.

"You've probably only got a fifty-fifty chance in the swamp anyway," she said.

Brown looked around at the Lincoln. It was dark. She could hear Sly and Craig talking, but they were out of sight.

"If you're going to go, go," she said.

He started backing away from her slowly, his hands still up, like he was pleading. That bothered her because it reminded her of Frank, the way he always looked like he was praying. He backed to the edge of the swamp, a shadow now, in a T-shirt and bikini underwear. He was starting to turn when she pulled the trigger, surprised by the noise and the way the gun jerked her hand. She saw his hands go down as he stumbled backwards, and she leveled the gun and fired again . . . and fired again.

Craig was there, standing beside her. "He ran," she said, and collapsed against him.

"His mother would be glad he was wearing red underwear," Sly said. "All that blood. She shot him right in the crotch, and again in the chest."

Julius had taken Colleen to the car. Craig stood on the road next to the Jeep when Sly came back from examining Brown. He watched as Sly wiped the gun clean. "Let's get out of here," Craig said. "There's a canal up the road where you can get rid of that."

* * *

They drove in silence back into Miami, Craig driving, Sly up front, Julius and Colleen in the back. It was nearly four o'clock in the morning when they reached the city.

"Where do you want the trunk?" Craig asked Sly.

"If we can stop by the bus, put it on there, then I can get out of this place, take it up to New York, where it's civilized."

Craig said, "Sly, I'm going to take Julius and Colleen over to Freeport on the boat. Let the old man play some roulette, give Colleen a chance to rest, figure out what she wants to do. She can put the money in a bank there where she doesn't have to explain anything."

"Sounds good."

"You want to go?"

"No. I've had enough of the tropics," Sly said.

Julius said, "They'll trace that car you rented. You thought about that?"

"I'm going to report it stolen as soon as we get back to Miami," Craig said.

Craig answered the phone in their room at the Carlyle the next morning at ten. It was Sly.

"Listen," Sly said. "I'm in a little trouble."

"You just got out of a little trouble."

"The vice cops picked me up on the beach the other day. You remember?"

"Yeah," Craig said. "It was only yesterday. Now what?"

"They came around the hotel looking for me. With a warrant. My record, they didn't have any problem getting one. For the bus too."

"No," Craig said.

"Yeah. They found the stuff."

"Where are you?"

"In jail. You're my one call."

"I'll come down; there's enough money to bail you out."

"No," Sly said. "I just realized I understand life in here. I got a few years left; I can enjoy myself. Outside, I'm getting hassled all the time."

"Sly—"

"Just tell Julius for me. He'll understand. Give my love to Colleen. And have a good time in the Bahamas."

Twenty-six

THEY SAT IN THE BAR OF THE GRAND BAHAMA PRINCESS Hotel in Freeport. From the outside the place looked like a replica of the Taj Mahal. Colleen Bishop, in a white cotton dress, a thin gold chain around her neck, sat in a wicker chair, sipping a rum punch. The noise from the casino drifted into the bar.

Craig said, "How much will you let him lose?"

Colleen smiled. "I gave him a stake of fifty grand. Told him not to lose it all at one table."

"You tell him about Sly?"

"Of course. It made perfect sense to Julius, fit right in with his cynical nature."

Half an hour later Julius came into the bar. He smiled at them, found a waiter and ordered an iced tea, and came back to their table. "Up five grand," he said. "What have I been playing, an hour and a half? Something like that."

"Quit," Colleen said. "Go back tomorrow."

He sipped his tea and lit a cigarette. "Listen," Julius said, "four hours, half a day. If I bring in ten grand, that's not bad for a guy who's retired. After five days you get your investment back. It beats waiting for a book on Meyer Lansky."

Julius sat for five minutes, finished his tea and got up. "I'm just taking a break," he said. "Back to work. Wish me luck."

They watched him walk back into the casino, excited as a young kid.

"Has he talked to you yet?" Craig asked.

"About what?"

He wondered why Julius hadn't told her. What was he waiting for?

"Nothing," Craig said. "I just thought he might have talked to you, that's all. About your life . . . what you're going to do."

She said, "Like a kid? People ask you what you're going to do when you grow up. I always thought I wanted to be a lawyer, a sort of hard-nosed, female Perry Mason but with a heart of gold." She laughed.

"I didn't mean it that way."

"But I'll tell you something. I learned something when I pulled that trigger. I thought I would feel guilty, probably have to spend the rest of my life living with nightmares. But I don't feel guilty and I don't think I'll have any nightmares. I'm glad I did it . . .

that Brown is dead. Maybe it isn't justice, but on a personal level . . . I think you know what I mean."

"Yeah," Craig said. "I know exactly what you mean." They sat there, a cool breeze blowing in off the ocean through the open shutters. They didn't talk for a while. Then Colleen looked at him. "What about you?" she asked. "What will you do?"

"Back to Miami, back to work, I guess."

"I'm going to pay you."

"For what?"

"You found Brown, didn't you? That's what you do, find people, you once told me."

"I don't want your money. It was a personal thing for me too. Besides, Frank paid me twenty-five thousand."

"Julius said Frank owed you another twenty-five. I want to stake you until you get back on your feet. I trust you," she said.

"I've got a better idea. Why don't you come to work for me?"

"A bounty hunter?"

"The first hard-nosed, female skip tracer. With a heart of gold. You'd be good at it."

Colleen laughed.

"I mean it," he said. "Try it for the summer. See what you think. I'll need a partner."

She looked at him, serious now, her eyes bright, aware. "Let's go see Julius, see what he thinks of the idea."

Colleen paid for the drinks. The two-note bleat of a siren filled the air as they got up from the table and suddenly died right outside the hotel. They walked back toward the casino as ambulance attendants wheeled in a stretcher. A crowd had formed around one of the tables.

Colleen said, "Oh, no. Don't let it be Julius." They worked their way through the crowd, pushing people aside, behind the medics.

Somebody shouted to give him air while another voice said the guy was already dead.

Pushing his way in, Craig looked down at the body slumped over the roulette table, his head on the green felt, spilled chips around his face. It was Julius.

A croupier said, "I think he had a heart attack. The guy had won over seven thousand dollars."

Colleen reached him as they were putting him on the stretcher. "No," she said. She put her hands on Julius's chest.

One of the medics pulled her back. "Are you related to him?"

Craig put an arm around her. "His daughter," he said.

Printed in the United States
By Bookmasters